Praise for Previous Work

"*My Sister Esther* moves quietly and skillfully.... impressive for its language, superb characterization and almost quiet desperation of day-to-day living, longing, wanting."
—*The Ottawa Xpress*

"Baillie's exploration of the family dynamic in action, especially the effect of parents on children, is admirable."
—*Books in Canada*

"Baillie skillfully evokes the unhappy childhood of sisters Esther and Muriel. [There is a] lyric quality of Baillie's prose.
—*Canadian Book Review Annual*

Madame Balashovskaya's Apartment

MADAME BALASHOVSKAYA'S APARTMENT

a novel by

Martha Baillie

To Peter Webb, whom I feel, erroneously, that I have known a long time! Best wishes, Martha Nov 30/99

TURNSTONE PRESS

Madame Balashovskaya's Apartment
copyright © 1999 Martha Baillie

Turnstone Press
607–100 Arthur Street
Artspace Building
Winnipeg, Manitoba
R3B 1H3
Canada R3B 1H3
www.TurnstonePress.com

All rights reserved. No part of this book may be reproduced or transmitted in any form or by any means—graphic, electronic or mechanical—without the prior written permission of the publisher. Any request to photocopy any part of this book shall be directed in writing to the Canadian Copyright Licensing Agency, Toronto.

Turnstone Press gratefully acknowledges the assistance of the Manitoba Arts Council, the Canada Council for the Arts and the Government of Canada through the Book Publishing Industry Development Program.

Canadä

Cover art: *Shadow on French Door*
Images® copyright 1999 PhotoDisc, Inc.

Design: Manuela Dias

Printed in Canada by
Friesens for Turnstone Press

Canadian Cataloguing in Publication Data

Baillie, Martha, 1960–

Madame Balashovskaya's apartment

ISBN 0-88801-235-7

I. Title.

PS8553.A3658 M34 1999   C813'.54   C99-920171-9
PR9199.3.B3425 M34 1999

For Jonno, my mother and Emma
À Christophe, Mamina et Lila.

Acknowledgements

My deepest gratitude goes to Jonno and Emma, and I thank my sister Christina for her affection, encouragement and insights. I thank Rosamund Owen, Theo Heras, Annie Beer, Mark Abley, Cary Fagan and Banuta Rubess for reading the manuscript at various stages, making invaluable suggestions and not allowing me to lose faith. Janet MacLean and Shelley Adler—thank you for examining certain scenes with expert eyes. I thank Geneviève Guillot for twenty years of friendship. Her generous hospitality, and that of Paul Guéring, made our stays in Paris possible. My mother, Greg Sharp, Anne Egger, Claire Dehenne, Theo Heras, Sarah Winters, and Ray and Sally all came to my rescue by caring for Emma and/or by providing me with a work space away from home. I am grateful to my co-workers at the Locke library for their support. The Bloor JCC offered me space in which to work. I am indebted beyond words to my editors Jennifer Glossop and Susan Goldberg for their knowledge, perspicacity, respect and diligence. I remain in awe of the courage and dedication of those who constitute Turnstone Press. The Ontario Arts Council provided me with much needed and relished support. Nourishment of all sorts came from many friends not mentioned here. I hope they know who they are and that their value is beyond measure.

Notre amour reste là	Our love stays put
Têtu comme une bourrique	Stubborn as a mule
Vivant comme le désir	Lively as desire
Cruel comme la mémoire	Cruel as memory
Bête comme les regrets	Foolish as regrets
Tendre comme le souvenir	Tender as remembrance
Froid comme le marbre	Cold as marble
Beau comme le jour	Beautiful as the day
Fragile comme un enfant	Fragile as a child
Il nous regarde en souriant	It looks at us, smiling
Et il nous parle sans rien dire	And it talks to us without speaking
Et moi je l'écoute en tremblant	And I listen to it, trembling
Et je crie	And I shout
. . .	. . .
Beaucoup plus tard au coin d'un bois	Much later in the corner of a wood
Dans la forêt de la mémoire	In the forest of memory
Surgis soudain	Appear suddenly
Tends-nous la main	Reach out your hand
Et sauve-nous.	And save us.
—Jacques Prévert	—Jacques Prévert, translated by M. Baillie.

One

In the late afternoon of Madame Eugénie Balashovskaya's ninetieth birthday, her guests celebrated. They filled her apartment with their words and cigarette smoke. Her plants were pushed to one side, as friends and relatives set down their plates and glasses. Behind the glass doors of the bookshelves, her books stood safe, if in no particular order. The brown surface of the piano shone, polished earlier that day by Josette, the concierge.

"The increasing number of immigrants . . ." said a male voice from the dining room. Whose voice is that? wondered Eugénie. She was seated on her green velvet settee, beneath her cousin's orange and blue portrait of Kiev. She opened her eyes. In all directions, her guests were lobbing words over invisible nets. Lips were blowing rings of smoke into the air.

Eugénie closed her eyes once more. She pictured her age as a cone of years, not unlike the cones of sugar her father had shown her long ago in his Kiev refinery. Tonight she was balancing carefully on the cone's rounded tip. From such a height she could barely hear what her guests were saying. At first this frustrated and then it relieved her. She dozed.

Far below the apartment, a boat laden with tourists pushed its way through the murky waters of the Seine. This boat shot a beam of cold light into the round dining room. The white light slipped along the curved wall and into the living room, over the piano, under the orange and purple domes of Kiev, out through the french doors and over the balcony wall.

As Eugénie opened her eyes, the boat's tinny music and glare glided away. She saw Anna, her slender young Canadian tenant, speaking with Nicholas, her grandson. Anna was Mary's daughter, but she possessed none of her mother's serenity. And why should she? She was all hunger and questions.

Eugénie leaned forward and through an effort of will caught Anna's words. She was explaining to Nicholas that a month ago she'd visited friends near Bremen, in Germany. Nicholas was correcting Anna's French.

"You didn't visit your friends but paid them a visit," he said. "A bee visits a flower, a man visits a woman's body. Do you see the difference from paying a visit? I expect you paid your friends in Germany a visit, but possibly there was someone there whom you visited as well?"

Eugénie watched Anna blush and wave her hands about. She saw her granddaughter Barbara step through the doorway from the dining room, catch sight of Nicholas and Anna, and retreat. Or had Barbara forgotten her napkin in the other room? Nothing more complicated than that?

"Private compassion is not enough. The Left must re-organize." The voice from the dining room belonged to Eugénie's son-in-law, Léon, Claire's husband. Eugénie strained to hear the rest of what Léon was saying about the Left but failed.

Why, Eugénie wondered, does this obstinate body of mine keep going? And what has happened to my first child, Rose? She should be here tonight, not I. But Rose had drowned, twenty years ago, in the Seine. "On purpose," Barbara still insisted. "Maman climbed up there and fell because she wanted to."

"No, the wind took her hat and she lost her balance," claimed Nicholas. But he knew no better than his sister. How could anyone prove a thing? Not even Mary, who was Rose's friend and had been standing on the bridge, had been able to make sense of Rose's death. But very little in this world makes sense and there is no other world, only the God that exists inside us, thought Eugénie. Our thoughts could be so helpful but often they are not.

Eugénie had chosen to keep her hair black. Her skin had an olive cast, and from the mole on her left cheek grew a coarse hair. From her upper lip, darker, finer hairs sprouted. She used a small pot of rouge to return to her cheeks the colour they'd lost. Whenever she opened her eyes wide, they became two blue pools of innocence.

A tongue of cold air entered the room. Eugénie found the source. Between the shoulders of cousins Clothilde and Berthe, young Anna was disappearing onto the balcony, pulling the tall doors shut behind her.

"*Quel froid!*" exclaimed several voices.

Eugénie wanted to call out, "Anna, you have no coat?" but tiredness assailed her. She did not stand up.

Anna is nineteen years old, Nicholas thirty-two, Barbara thirty-four, Claire fifty-eight, calculated Eugénie. How is it I have a daughter so old? I have survived nine-tenths of a century. So many numbers we keep track of. The weight of her eyelids pulled them down; the noisy room drifted away.

BESIDE THE PIANO stood Nicholas, holding a bowl of ice cream and listening to his sister. He rarely knew what to say to Barbara, how to please her. He'd tried a small confiding smile, an electric look, a penetrating gaze, but none of these had charmed or soothed her. And so he ate his dessert, shivering in the cold cascade of his sister's words that flowed across the floor.

Nicholas remembered the dream he'd had the night before.

A flock of white birds had alighted on a tree by the bank of a fast-moving river. The tree, as though covered with huge white blossoms, stood trembling at the noisy water's edge. Then all at once the birds flew off, leaving the tree dark and naked. He'd woken in a panic, sweating. Perhaps he was the tree and the white birds every woman he'd ever known? As Nicholas emerged from these thoughts, Barbara's long, pale neck came into focus. He saw her gulp for air.

"I was cleaning the walls," she said, "preparing to paint them, and I came down from the ladder to answer the door. It was him again. He wanted to borrow a lemon—or so he claimed. I suppose all concierges drink, but why must he pick on me? I tell you I can't stand it anymore."

As NICHOLAS AND BARBARA walked into the dining room, Eugénie Balashovskaya pulled herself from her green settee and followed them. Her gaze swept over the platters of food. A smoked trout lay untouched on a bed of lettuce. She divided the fish into days. I won't have to shop for weeks, she said to herself.

"You're not to live on leftovers, Mémère," Nicholas announced, stepping away from his sister and slipping his arm through his grandmother's. "On Wednesday I'm coming to inspect your refrigerator for suspicious bowls wrapped in cellophane. And what are you doing standing? Especially on your birthday. Let me get you a chair." He set off through the tangle of guests towards an unoccupied chair.

Had Nicholas seen her eye divide the trout, or had he heard her thinking? Eugénie believed the ache in her leg was a thought. "God is Mind." So her father had told her, oh so long ago, when the first cars sputtered through Paris. "God is Mind." Occasionally her father's watch, resting on his paunch, ticked in her ear, hooves clopped, trampling the present into the pavement in seconds. Memories are not trustworthy friends unless tamed, she said to herself. Only trapped, trained memories are harmless. These entertain like hamsters that we bring out for guests. They run in circles within a little wheel inside their cage, and everyone finds them charming—delightful little memories. Even so, a rodent event or sentence will sometimes scurry from a dark corner, twitching its nose. Eugénie resolved to beat all threatening recollections away with a broom.

Nicholas returned with the chair, holding it upright by its legs, above the heads of her guests. He smiled, a broad smile intended for his grandmother alone.

A throne for a bride, thought Barbara.

"Will you really come on Wednesday to inspect my refrigerator?" Eugénie asked him. "If you do, you must stay for coffee. It will be peaceful. Only Claire will be here. She comes every Wednesday afternoon."

"I will try my best but I can't promise. Don't spend your party longing for Wednesday." He sliced some cheese, placed it on a piece of bread and handed it to his grandmother. "You must promise me, Mémère, that you will climb the stairs to the rue de Passy every day for your groceries. All those stairs, those stairs you detest, they are a gift. Without them you would have no legs."

BARBARA STUDIED NICHOLAS from a safe distance. He was not a tall man. A dark, luxurious moustache grew beneath his nose. If he were to shave his moustache off, wondered Barbara, would it reappear in the morning, the same size?

Nicholas caught her eye and she felt him inviting her to laugh, to see life as a glorious puzzle, but she did not give in. She adjusted the Italian plate hanging on her grandmother's wall. To you, Nicholas, I am a letter in an equation. You consider us all examples of this and that, tidbits within your theories.

The sudden cold made Barbara turn. It was Anna, coming in from the balcony.

"Those stairs hurt my legs, especially my ankles. Or rather

it is my thinking that is the trouble. I have an undisciplined mind and that is why I feel pain," said Eugénie.

"The stairs keep your legs strong," said Nicholas. "Without them you would be stuck in this apartment like a bird in a cage." He took out a cigarette, lighted it, and added, "Save me from birds."

"Why, birds are lovely!" said Barbara.

"I've had birds and blossoming trees filling my mind all evening," explained Nicholas. "If I utter the word 'bird' once more, toss me out the door."

"With pleasure."

Barbara crossed the room and crouched by her grandmother. She took one quick breath and asked, "What can I do for you, Mémère?"

"Nothing. You can do nothing for me, *ma petite*."

"You're right. I can't do a thing." Barbara's face became a sinking ship, the captain watching from far away in a rubber dinghy.

"Barbara, *ma petite*—" Eugénie began but stopped. She felt a leak spring inside herself at the sight of her granddaughter sinking. "You must not take everything I or anyone says so much to heart." The words, cut loose, floated away.

Nicholas lifted a fork from the table and twirled it between his palms.

"And where else can words go but to the heart, Maman?" asked Claire, entering the dining room. She had been listening to their conversation from the living room, wanting to join them but unable to free herself from her husband Léon's disputation on the church's plans to destroy secular education. Now was her chance.

She said, "Soon the escalator will be done, Maman. It will go all the way up to the rue de Passy. They are promising it for May. Then you won't have to climb all those steps." Claire raised her hand to the nape of her neck, where that morning the hairdresser had snipped her grey hair, leaving it short as a boy's. Her eyes were also grey. Her voice was what people remembered the best. It flowed uphill, tinkled at the top, sparkled in the air before tumbling.

Claire now spotted solitary Anna, Canadian Anna, in the sitting room eating an orange. She smiled, but Anna's gaze was fixed on the piano.

"Escalator?" asked Eugénie.

"I'm so sorry," said Claire. "The moment has passed and now I've interrupted. The stairs, Maman, you said that climbing them makes your legs ache." Claire bent at the waist, caught the scent of her mother's perfume. She kissed the top of her mother's head then added, "I wanted to say something earlier but couldn't because Léon was talking. He is like a submarine and does not need to come up for air."

"Léon is forever talking. It's a well-known fact," declared Léon, who had followed his wife into the dining room.

"Léon, you know I don't say it to hurt you but because it is true. You love to talk. It gives you pleasure." Claire pressed her husband's hand in hers.

"I couldn't imagine Claire causing anyone pain." Barbara's face brightened as she looked into her aunt's eyes.

"And I say the escalator will be completed by next September at the earliest," proclaimed Léon, taking a pen from his pocket. "Do you have a paper, Mémère? I'll draw you a diagram of the government's soul."

"Léon. When did you become a believer in souls?" teased Nicholas, smoothing his moustache.

"Barbara has accepted a proposal of marriage," announced Eugénie in her largest, most joyous voice.

The strawberries sat on the table, brilliant red. White napkins opened in a fan. Gold coffee spoons balanced in tiny saucers.

First, those nearest Eugénie Balashovskaya fell silent, then all ears and eyes turned to the dining room. Someone's knee creaked as he shifted his weight. Cousin Clothilde coughed. Léon clicked his pen shut.

Nicholas turned to his sister. "What splendid news." He offered her everything, an electric look, a small smile, his thick moustache perfectly trimmed. He kissed her on either cheek, then raised his glass. "Ladies and gentlemen, to Barbara."

"How could you, Mémère?" cried Barbara, and she ran from the room.

Two

CLAIRE SAT BESIDE HER MOTHER on the voluminous blue sofa named Mitterrand. It was Nicholas who had given the piece of furniture its name, in the hope of a truer republic to come. The Left had been gaining in popularity the previous year, and Nicholas hoped 1981 would see them elected.

Eugénie's knitting needles clicked. A red sleeve grew from the needles and spread across her knees. There was the ticking of clocks and the silent breathing of the plants. From the street far below came the sound of a shovel scraped across gravel.

It was the Wednesday following Eugénie's birthday party, and Claire was thinking about time running out and time running in. Why hadn't Barbara wanted the rest of the family to know of her engagement? Maman had chosen her moment poorly. But everyone had heard of Henri, even if no one had met him. Were Rose still alive, how would she handle Barbara? Had Rose survived, would her daughter have become such a secretive and unpredictable woman? We are all thinking about Rose more than usual and asking ourselves unanswerable questions because of Anna, decided Claire. The three clocks struck four, and Eugénie's needles continued their clicking, twisting and binding the red wool.

"I should be going home soon." Claire got up from the sofa.

"Oh, but you mustn't leave yet," insisted Eugénie. She inched forward, pulling then pushing the sofa's blue arm, and succeeded in standing. "I have something to show you."

"Sit down, Maman. Tell me what you want to show me, and I'll bring it here."

"You can't bring it to me." Eugénie laughed. "We'll go and look together. I've planted a persimmon for Barbara. And my tomatoes are nearing two inches tall."

With the obstinacy of a tugboat, Eugénie disappeared behind the sitting-room door. Claire followed. In the living room, Eugénie yanked the stiff handle of the tall balcony doors. She advanced into the city's roar.

"Do you see, Claire, how strong they look?" She pointed to the seedlings growing in the warmth of the glass box beside her feet.

At night she covered the box with a blanket to protect it from frost. So far the winter was proving mild and her plants were thriving. In the summer she would give them to her gardener to plant behind her small house at Arcelon.

"They're splendid, Maman."

Claire pressed her back against the broad stone railing. It felt hard and solid.

Since taking early retirement a year ago from her position as senior engineer with the firm Dupont and Latour, she'd become fearless. No longer satisfied just to dabble her toes, she'd waded into the stream of poetry, politics, philosophy and music which had been gurgling past her since her childhood. Various currents caressed her shins, as she walked along the muddy bottom. She'd begun questioning everything. She'd arrived at a new certainty that all was uncertain. The laws of engineering belonged to another world. This realization frightened and exhilarated her. When she spoke to Léon of the waters in which she was swimming, he called her his "lovely mermaid."

But to whom did she owe the greatest loyalty? To Léon,

Mémère or her new interests? The three vied with each other mercilessly for her time and attention.

She had looked after her mother as long as she could remember. This involved, of late, staring at the skin that sagged between her mother's knuckles, then examining the taut green surface of a leaf on one of her mother's plants, until the details of both skin and leaf filled her with awe. Only then did the coil of frustration inside her unwind. Only then did she forget she must choose between loyalties.

Claire looked down at the tiny plants growing under their glass roof. There, she thought, is my mother's curling green will to live.

In the alcove off the dining room the telephone rang. Worse than its singing the same note over and over, thought Eugénie, is its unspoken threat to stop at any moment. Then we will not know who called. Eugénie looked about her for something to hold. She chose her daughter's arm. They set out across the living-room carpet, Eugénie scowling.

"Shall I answer it?" offered Claire.

"No. You're too kind, *ma chérie*," replied Eugénie without lifting her head, concentrating on her task, the patterned carpet passing slowly under her feet.

The ringing persisted until Eugénie arrived. She sat down on the straight wooden chair, facing the telephone.

"*Allô?*"

"Mémère, I can't live here any longer."

Barbara was not crying, but she gulped for air.

"What is it, *ma petite?*"

"This man is crazy. He's come to my door three times today—first to inspect the windows, then to borrow another lemon. Ten minutes later he realized he couldn't live without sugar and returned. I haven't let him in. I'm frightened, Mémère. What am I to do if he comes again?"

"Have you told him you don't wish to be disturbed?"

"He doesn't care, Mémère. He's dangerous."

CLAIRE TILTED HER HEAD back and saw that the sky was plastered with grey clouds. She had escaped to the balcony so as not to overhear her mother's conversation. Since Claire's retirement, her intimacy with her mother had grown, and with it a desire to respect her mother's privacy. Eugénie, all of her abilities imperceptibly yet irrevocably fraying, was losing so much else. The sky looks bandaged, thought Claire. Perhaps it's cracked or ailing? I have no umbrella. She shook her head, pleased by its lightness, now her hair was so short. Maman probably has an old umbrella I can borrow. I'll step out and buy her a few groceries. Barbara may keep her hostage on the phone for hours.

A string shopping bag proved to be hanging from the handle of the kitchen door, and with it a collapsible green umbrella. That is the problem in this family, decided Claire, unhooking them both. We all think we know everything about each other. Perhaps this time Barbara's not in trouble.

The apartment's heavy door closed behind Claire, and she walked along the red carpet past the broad staircase to the small elevator. It arrived with a whirr followed by a groan, and a clank.

"I TELL YOU, MÉMÈRE, I can't stand it any longer. He makes me so nervous, I'm afraid I'll fall off my ladder. I'm not going to paint my living room. I'm going to put away my ladder and all the paint I bought. Because of this odious man, I'll have to keep living in a green apartment. I am to be surrounded forever by a horrible colour chosen by my brother."

"Shouldn't you call the police?" suggested Eugénie.

"And tell them to arrest a man for asking me for a lemon? How could I, Mémère? It's bad enough the family thinks I'm mad."

"Who, *ma petite*? Who has called you mad?"

"Not to my face, Mémère. Nobody will say so. They don't want to risk being impolite."

"I will make up a bed. You must spend the night with me, here."

"Oh, Mémère, I'd love to but I can't leave. I'm expecting an important phone call."

"Shall I pack an overnight bag and come to you?" Eugénie looked down, expecting to see that her shoes had grown larger. Their weight made her ankles ache. She counted the steps in her head, preparing herself for the journey on the Métro, all the way to Barbara's. Twenty. Twenty stairs will bring me level with the Passy station. At Charles de Gaulle Étoile, thirty steps down, then the endless passageway and at Stalingrad more corridors and escalators. I will be jostled, she thought.

"Yes, Mémère. Yes. Come." Barbara's lungs released the air they had been clutching. "I'm sending you a thousand kisses, Mémère."

"Then I send you one thousand and three," murmured Eugénie.

"Thank you, Mémère. I'd come for you but my stupid car is in the garage."

"Don't fret, Barbara. There is the Métro."

"You believe me, don't you, about the lemon?"

"Of course. Why invent such a story?"

On the dining-room mantelpiece the clock struck five. It was made of black marble and guarded by two gilded angels.

"Nicholas doesn't believe me. I'm sure of it."

"Your brother does not like things to appear too simple."

"Except Maman's death—that he's happy enough to simplify."

Eugénie straightened her spine. Sleep reached for her without tact or pity, but did not win. Her head tilted for a moment. Barbara, she thought, if only you could find more interesting work than typing letters of response to the complaints that rain down on the Samaritaine department store. Once in a while, your work becomes colourful, you say. A fierce discontent arrives, scribbled in crayon on the remains of a box of tissue, and to this you must compose an answer. Then the dull, pale letters follow, page after page. A pillowcase has torn, pyjamas do not fit, and the fault belongs to the Samaritaine. If only, *ma petite*, you could find a job that used your mind.

"Mémère, it's all so very complicated."

"Nicholas is interested in what is complicated. Perhaps if it is tangled or elaborate, you should speak with him."

"I don't want Nicholas to know anything more about my life than I've been stupid enough to tell him already."

"Very well. Very well. You must do as you think best. You must trust in your heart." You must find work that engages your heart and this man will stop asking you for lemons, Eugénie thought. Her eyelids grew heavy. As they dropped, they hid the grey telephone. She tasted dust on her tongue. The alcove off the dining room vanished.

The summer road was narrow and bordered by yellow fields of rape seed. Barbara's black hair hung in two braids, each secured by a blue ribbon tied in a bow. Her small hot hand clutched Eugénie's. Nicholas, seated on the ground in front of them, drew in the dirt with a stick. Rose yawned. Their eight legs and forty toes were covered in dust. The sky, by some miracle, had remained clean and blue.

"Stop. I must take your picture," Rose announced, wrestling with the buckle of her overnight bag.

Eugénie inadvertently shook her foot and the grey telephone's orderly face reappeared. No, she thought, that's not what Rose would have said. Is it possible I've already forgotten how my daughter spoke? She successfully willed the telephone away.

"Would you mind, Mother, if we stopped a moment longer? I'd like to take a picture."

"Barbara, Nicholas, are you thirsty?" And Rose extracted a flask of water from her bag. In the dirt, Nicholas drew snakes and lions. Barbara watched her mother unscrew the lid of the flask. The sky was a single shade of infinite blue.

Yes, decided Eugénie with relief, that is how Rose spoke.

Eugénie opened her eyes.

"Trust? You want me to trust? If you hadn't blurted out at the party what I told you in confidence, they wouldn't know I am going to be married," Barbara was shouting into the telephone. "Now they'll be watching, waiting for my marriage to fail."

"I am profoundly sorry, *ma petite*." What did I miss while I was dreaming? Eugénie wondered. I've missed something.

"You nearly ruined my happiness."

"Barbara, forgive me." It is true, Barbara, we watch you— the outside of you, Eugénie thought, then reprimanded herself. This is not Right Thinking.

"I forgive you," murmured Barbara, innocent and tiny now.

"Barbara, I have another question to ask, though I've no right to pry. If you and Henri are to be married, why are you repainting your apartment? Soon you'll be moving somewhere larger."

"How can you ask me such a question? I've already told you. I want it to look beautiful. Is that wrong? And who told you, Mémère, that we plan to move? I never told you that."

"Would there be room for both of you?"

"Mémère, I don't want to discuss this. Are you coming? I'm frightened."

"Straight away."

"I *am* going to be married."

"Of course you are."

"And when my car is out of the garage I'll take you to Arcelon. And when summer finally comes and it stops being grey and rainy every day we'll plant your tomatoes. Doesn't the air smell lovely at Arcelon? Especially in the mornings. Don't you think so?"

"Yes, Barbara."

"Are you coming soon?"

Their conversation ended. A dry click severed her granddaughter from her. Empty air. I will take my hairbrush, toothbrush, nightgown. So much to brush. Another of God's lessons?

Or one of his jokes? I will go and put them in the bag now. But where is Claire? How rude I have been! Claire?

And Eugénie Balashovskaya closed her eyes. Sleep came, merciful sleep. There was no dream at first. Then large and unannounced as a summer cloud, a dream drifted in.

EUGÉNIE LOWERED THE TRAIN WINDOW and stuck her head into the hot, dry air of Greece.

"Eugénie!" her mother warned.

She pulled her head into the safe, stuffy compartment.

That evening, while her mother dozed, she again stuck her head out the window and heard the cicadas rubbing their wings. Somewhere there was a war. The year was 1914 and the month September. Eugénie had attained the age of twenty-four. In a town called Sarajevo, a prince had been shot. Eugénie and her mother had left Paris in a hurry. They had sent a letter to Papa; but who could tell if the envelope would reach Kiev. Even in the dark the lemons hanging from the rows of trees offered her their pure yellow. It was night and the train was approaching Thessaloniki. In an orchard beside the tracks raced rows of lemon trees. She leaned out. The light from the rushing windows of the train swept over the fruit, and their colour exploded. The weight of the lemons was pulling the branches to the ground. She reached her arm into the hot, dry night. The train raced on, left the lemons behind. The train reached Thessaloniki and ground to a halt, its engine steaming and hissing, while passengers scrambled. Then the train carried Eugénie and her mother out of Thessaloniki. In Athens they would board a ship. Then another train and another.

"I hope," said her mother, "your father sends the car to the station." Theirs was one of the first cars in Kiev.

"How will he know which train we're on?"

"He will have to send the car for every train."

Her mother removed her glasses which were pinching the

bridge of her nose. "This tea is not properly brewed," she remarked.

Then the passengers, not only in Eugénie's compartment but in others as well, took out their instruments. The cellist and the viola player stood in the corridor. They played Mozart's String Quartet in D Minor. The faster Eugénie's bow sliced back and forth across the strings of her violin the smaller her mother became, until the woman shrank so small as to be hidden by the silver bridge of her own spectacles. The spectacles hopped about on the seat, Eugénie's mother gone.

"Maman, you're sleeping," said Claire, jiggling her mother's arm until Eugénie opened her eyes. "I must be off, Maman, but I didn't want to leave without telling you. There are groceries in the kitchen—a loaf of rye bread and a piece of goat cheese, also some apples."

"Was I sleeping? How rude of me." Eugénie gripped the table and with her other hand pushed down on the chair. She knew where she'd left her purse.

"What are you trying to get, Maman?"

"My purse."

"I won't accept a penny for the groceries," said Claire, and kissed her mother's powdery cheek.

Eugénie was standing. She had not been defeated. She didn't need her purse now, but hadn't really expected to. She took her daughter's arm.

"Can you drive me to Barbara's?" she asked. "If you can't, you must say so and I will take the Métro."

Three

Claire's car vanished from the street below. Barbara helped Mémère off with her coat and hung it from a hook on the green wall.

This has been a good apartment for Barbara, thought Eugénie. The rent is low and she has taken pleasure from the view of the canal. Was it seven years ago that Nicholas passed it on to her? Seven years since he and Janine married? Now he and Janine have divorced and Barbara is to marry.

Eugénie sat down on one of Barbara's three hard chairs and asked, "When will I meet your Henri?"

Barbara's three dolls observed Eugénie from their seats beneath the window. They stared through her with glass eyes that contained layers of unchanging expression. Their delicate porcelain hands rested at their sides. Elegant clothes were buttoned over their sawdust-filled bodies. Eugénie fished in her mind for their names, without success. She rested her own stiff hands on the smooth vinyl surface of her brown overnight bag, which lay in her lap. She had found the sturdy little bag at the supermarket and paid a minimum for it. This pleased her. She set the bag on the floor beside her feet then reached up and smoothed her wiry hair.

"Soon Mémère, I will introduce you to my Henri. I promise. Let me look at you, Mémère. Lower your hand. There, you look lovely. Let me take your bag. I'm glad you've come. Thank you."

"Does he have a vocation?" asked Eugénie.

Barbara turned away. Her books stood pressed against each other on the narrow shelves beside the living room door. She hurried past them.

"I've already told you, Mémère," she shouted from the kitchen, "he's an administrator with Renault. He's mine." She returned with a plate of biscuits which she set on the table. "At last I have someone, Mémère, besides you, who loves me!" She noticed she was shouting and lowered her voice. "Why should I trot him up and down for them to appraise? They don't want to believe that someone could love me."

"Who, *ma petite*, does not wish to believe?"

"I am ugly."

"You are not ugly, Barbara."

"No, I am not ugly to look at. But I'm full of ugliness. Sometimes, Mémère, I can taste it. My own ugliness coats my tongue."

She handed a cup of tea to her grandmother, a biscuit balanced on the saucer.

"And your Henri? For him you are beautiful."

"But he's not here." Barbara waved at the window, as though Henri had been sucked through it.

"Where has he gone?"

"On a business trip to London. He'll be away for two weeks."

"Such a short time? He'll be back before you know it."

"No, Mémère. I will fill with slime. He won't come back. I tell myself that soon we'll be married and I'll stop worrying and all will be golden, but it won't. By the time he returns from London he won't want me."

To still her hands, Barbara sank her fingers into her hair,

close to her scalp, and tugged. Her hair, like Nicholas's and Eugénie's, was dark and thick, resilient. She had her mother's wide grey eyes and broad cheek bones, her father's pale skin. Her scalp tingled agreeably from the tugging. She looked about the room. In the corner sat her basket of sewing scraps. She moved to the basket, crouched down and started to fold the bits of material into tidy bundles that she laid in rows on the floor. Brown striped silk, flowered pink cotton, blue wool. She looked up from her soothing task, studied her grandmother, and frowned.

"You have not touched your tea, Mémère."

"Claire and I took tea together before we came. I cannot drink another drop."

"Why didn't you say so? What am I to do with all this tea?" She didn't wait for an answer. She was tired of waiting. Waiting to find courage. Waiting for Henri to become someone he wasn't. Leaping up, she grabbed the tea things and marched to the kitchen. She glared at the teapot then dumped its contents into the sink.

"HAVE YOU ANY NEW costume designs to show me?" asked Eugénie, when Barbara had cleared the table after dinner.

"Yes. For *Uncle Vanya*. They aren't all done yet. But one of them... You'll see... Or you may not like it."

Only to Mémère would she show her work. That made Mémère all the more important and dangerous. She untied the black ribbons and slid her drawings from their stiff folder.

"Vanya's suit has to be missing a button. He has forgotten an important part of himself," she explained, spreading out the drawings with the samples of material pinned to them. "Vanya is in decline. And the suit had to be of a pale grey cloth to echo the colour of his mother's dress, only hers I wanted smooth, and for him little lumps and knots."

Eugénie held the drawing with care, tilted it into the light.

"I don't like the doctor's hat. It hasn't worked," continued Barbara. "I can't get it right." She was staring over Eugénie's shoulder, frowning. "Astrov is difficult."

"You have captured Vanya. It seems so to me," said Eugénie, smiling. "But I understand so little about these matters. What do you think, *ma petite*? Couldn't you show these to someone in one of the theatres?"

"I didn't make them to show to anyone. Can nothing be private? Why does everyone else's opinion matter? Don't I have one of my own?" retorted Barbara, and she gathered up her work, returning it to its thin hiding place. "And if I make them out of love, is that silly? Do they have to be judged in order to exist fully?"

Mémère yawned, and was filled with irritation at her crumbling body's inability to stay awake at crucial moments. I must concentrate, she told herself, take charge of my mind, rid my soul of this ungodly exhaustion and impatience.

"If Maman were alive, I would show these drawings to her," said Barbara, pressing her palms down on her knees. She was seated once more at her grandmother's feet. "And Maman could show me her designs for buildings. She didn't show them to me when I was growing up. She didn't speak much of her plans for buildings, her blueprints, did she? But I'm sure Ivan Sherbatsky showed her plenty of his horrible paintings and expected her to admire them."

"Were they horrible? I found them confusing, but Claire and Léon adored his work and expected it would be recognized one day."

"The portrait of a giraffe, the one he gave Maman, Claire and Léon have it hanging in their guest room. It is ugly. Why did she have to fall in love with him? He was so scrawny and pale, and he smelled of pickles. How could she want him?"

"I remember him as smelling sweet, of beets perhaps."

"Mémère, how can you say such a thing? Doesn't it matter to you? She was your daughter . . ."

Eugénie stared down at her own feet, frowning, as if her shoes were not her own. With a stubborn slowness, she lifted her head.

"You're right, Barbara. She could have chosen better. But it was all a long time ago. And we don't know..."

"Well, I blame him. She's dead, not just because of my father but because of Ivan Sherbatsky and Mary Bertram. And now Mary's daughter, Anna, has come, and you are letting her live with you."

"Anna is studying at the Sorbonne. Mary wrote from Canada and asked if I knew of a room to rent. It is not easy in Paris to find affordable lodgings."

"She didn't have to come to Paris. Why must I be polite to her? Nicholas will seduce her. She's Mary's daughter, after all. Even Claire finds her charming. It's horrible, Mémère. I tell you, I can't stand it."

Eugénie touched her handkerchief to the corner of her mouth. She groped for answers to Barbara's questions and found none. Her heavy eyebrows drew together. She did not wish to speculate about Rose's death. Not anymore.

She recalled Sherbatsky as smelling of beets, boiled and sweet. But it was true that when he came for lunch, he gobbled up all the pickles she served, leaving none for anyone else. A Russian lost in Paris, a skinny fledgling from the Moscow Art Institute, he'd come to her clutching a letter of introduction from his revered professor, Zalman Balashovsky, her cousin. The year was 1958. His explanation of how he'd escaped the Soviet Union was lacy, a work of artistry, of fine threads and knots, with plenty of holes. She had invited him to lunch and Mary as well, and of course Rose and the children were there. Some months later, Rose and Sherbatsky fell in love. She did not ask Rose if Sherbatsky planned to mary her. She was not so indiscreet. François, the children's father, had left shortly before Ivan appeared, and that was a good thing. Rose, Sherbatsky, and Mary. The three became inseparable. Rose was loved.

Eugénie's ankles ached. Why this incessant living in the past? I must resist, she told herself, straightening her spine. For Barbara, all this remembering is a certain path to unhappiness. We must address the present. God exists only in the here and now, in our expression of him.

She drew her eyebrows together, preparing for the storm she was about to cause. If thunder must clap, let it do so in the present.

She said, "Your concierge has been no trouble since I've arrived. Perhaps he has calmed down?"

"No doubt he's been eating supper. But he hasn't given up, Mémère."

"You don't think so?"

"It's not a matter of what I think. I know he hasn't given up. Tomorrow he'll appear at my door again. Sometimes, Mémère, you can be so naïve." Barbara twisted a strand of her hair around her finger, as though mooring a boat.

"Claire also tells me I am naïve," mused Eugénie.

"You trust too easily. Perhaps that is why you trust me."

"Why shouldn't I trust you?"

"Oh, Mémère, you'll never understand. How am I to live through the next twelve days? That man will call. He lets up only when he sees Henri's car parked in the street or if he knows that someone is here."

"You must be strong and open yourself to what is beautiful, *ma petite*. What is good and beautiful will fill you. If you can bring yourself to pray that will also help, although I know you do not believe in God."

"Mémère, I'm quite exhausted. Shouldn't we go to bed?"

Four

NICHOLAS KELMAN, STUCK IN HIS WHITE CAR on the Pont Notre-Dame, felt himself being slowly digested by the serpent of traffic slumbering on the bridge. His aim was to cross the river to the Hôtel-Dieu, where in fifteen minutes he was expected to attend the monthly meeting of the hospital's psychiatric staff. The meeting will begin without me, thought Nicholas. I will be forgiven by some but not by others.

The snake wriggled in its sleep, and Nicholas was able to advance a few feet. Again the car in front of him stopped, and the long serpent lay motionless, digesting its meal of Parisians. When I arrive late, predicted Nicholas, Dr. Philippe Grandet will take note.

It was five-thirty and the damp, grey sky was draining of light. The grimy wall of the old hospital was punctured by rows of windows that glowed yellow. Along the bridge at regular intervals, lamps perched on ornate poles cast circles of a colder light on to the pavement.

On the seat beside Nicholas lay a large brown envelope containing his manuscript. "Mental Cost and the Organization of Work" by Dr. Nicholas Kelman. The morning mail had returned it, decorated with an appreciative note of rejection.

"How's the book coming along?" Grandet will ask after the meeting, thought Nicholas. "I don't imagine the fantasies of the working class can be terribly varied?"

Nicholas imagined asking Grandet, "What hope is there of happiness within a society that is not founded upon the liberation of mental life?" He would go on from there: "Publishers with budgets to balance are always suspicious of a new field." Nicholas ran his fingers along the surface of the envelope and pictured the field he'd stepped into as vast, covered by a thin layer of fresh snow.

The driver of the car in front of him started to scratch at the skin behind his left ear.

"Monsieur Citröen," Nicholas addressed the unknown driver with the itchy ear, "you don't wish to take into account the mental lives of your workers, do you? The tendons and backs of your workers cause you trouble enough. Who am I to tell you about their anxieties, their fantasies? Your workers assure you that they are not anxious. How convenient to believe them."

Immobilized on the Pont Notre-Dame, Nicholas longed for the results of his research to spread, to affect legislation. When would his name travel down the Seine and cross oceans? Through the car window, through the elaborate metal railing of the bridge, he watched the waters of the river rise in small directionless waves. Each wave was fast replaced by another that swished from side to side.

If he could get across the bridge in the next five minutes and park the car without difficulty, he might arrive on time. To hell with Grandet.

The driver of the car in front reached into the passenger seat and lifted something to his face. Why didn't I eat more at lunch? regretted Nicholas. He looked down at the brown envelope on the seat beside him. His favourite case was that of the shop foreman.

"Sit down, Grandet," said Nicholas, and pointed to an imaginary stool raised a few inches from the floor of the car. "I have a tale to tell you."

"In a small provincial town live a foreman and his wife. Though the foreman finds his work satisfying, his wife urges him to change occupations. She is a hairdresser and considers her husband's factory job a source of social shame. In her campaign to sway her husband, she enlists the help of friends and family, all of whom inhabit the same provincial town. The foreman, surrounded, succumbs. He abandons his factory and finds work in an insurance office. Deprived of physical labour, the fellow experiences intense anxiety. He starts playing soccer on the weekends, soon evenings as well. All day he slides files stuffed with paper into drawers; as the sun sets, his heart pounding, he chases a black and white ball across a stretch of muddy grass. But soccer does not save him.

"His new life, clean and sedate, becomes unbearable. The structure of his personality collapses. The poor fellow takes to barking at plants. Found on all fours in the kitchen, devouring the petals of a potted violet, he informs his family he is obeying the dictates of a voice. He crawls about the house, grazing on all greenery within reach. After several weeks of this, his family comes to their wits' end. They drag him off to the hospital. A treatment of strong neuroleptics dispels the psychosis, but not until he returns to his physically demanding work as shop foreman does he stop experiencing intense anxiety.

"How do you explain this, Grandet?" Nicholas asked the dashboard. He tugged at his moustache. He found himself smiling. "Take your time, *mon cher* Grandet. We are stuck in traffic."

There was now room for Nicholas's car to roll three feet forwards. Had he looked out his side window at that moment, he would have seen Anna walking along the bridge in her sturdy walking shoes and a green corduroy skirt. But he failed to turn his head.

ANNA'S RED-GOLD HAIR hung to her waist. It needed a trim. She walked quickly, feeling superior to the people stuck in their cars. She glanced with amused pity into the stationary vehicles. In one unassuming white car, the driver, without warning, became Nicholas.

It was him. She recognized his profile. For a moment she held herself still, then she ran. Between two green wooden boxes strapped to the wall above the river, two boxes from which old books and postcards were sold during the day, Anna hid. She imagined Nicholas rolling down his window and taking her face in his hands. But instead of kissing her, he scowled. She explained that she had not come on purpose, that when she set out to cross the Pont Notre-Dame she could not have known that he would be stuck there in his car.

The idea of Nicholas kissing her terrified her. She considered her own sexual desires fierce and destructive. Was it from her mother she'd learned this? Anna couldn't decide. She knew that if no boy had ever kissed her, it was because something hidden inside her made her undesirable.

On those Friday nights when Mémère invited Nicholas to dinner and he sat across from Anna, she felt his eyes gather her details into a bouquet, his careful attention change her into someone lovely. The pleasure of this frightened her.

To calm herself, Anna imagined him as a young boy. Shortly before she'd come to Paris, her mother had shown her a snapshot of Nicholas, aged eleven. His shoulders and thin chest were naked, his dark shorts held up by a worn leather belt. His hair was cut very short, and he seemed to Anna the solemn prisoner of some grave unhappiness.

That boy no longer existed, she knew. But she concentrated upon him when Nicholas came to dinner. She saw, in this man in front of her, the boy freed of his sadness, and this made her want to kiss him, to celebrate his liberty.

To escape these fantasies, Anna reminded herself that Nicholas was a doctor with an office, that people paid him for his opinions. "I will ask Nicholas," Mémère would say, with pride. "But he is very busy. We won't eat until eight, or if he arrives late we will eat at nine."

Such a man couldn't find me interesting or desirable, Anna convinced herself, fighting against her senses.

The very first time Anna sat across the table from Nicholas, they had talked about sculpture. His voice and his eyes lifted her so that she spilled over her rim and into the round dining room. And he didn't tell her to contain herself but drank her in with a look of confident yet bewildered pleasure. She became, for an eternal moment, liquid. He gave a sigh of puzzled satisfaction, then spoke her name, "Anna," as though he were dreaming her into existence and had done so often, before they'd met. Next, he pulled himself from his reverie and laughed and said, "*Sacrée*, Anna. How did you learn all that?" an ironic smile dancing on his lips.

"I read it in a book about Rodin."

"It was at the Musée Rodin that I lost the bracelet Sonya gave me," interjected Eugénie. "I hunted for it in the garden, on all fours, under every rosebush and tree."

He thinks I am a child, Anna decided. He examines every woman as he did me, a moment ago. For him this is a game. My innocence amuses him. Very well. I don't care.

But Nicholas's smile had softened as he watched Anna lift her fork to her mouth, and her defiance withered. By the evening's end, all that mattered to her was when she might see him again.

ANNA EMERGED FROM HER HIDING place and walked until she came to a flight of stairs leading down to the water's edge. She descended and continued beside the river, then sat down on a stone bench. Is he still stuck up there, on the Pont Notre-Dame? she wondered. Could he have seen me? In the dark water of the Seine, the lighted windows of elegant apartments rippled. High above her head, a few dead leaves, clinging to the poplars, rustled. She took from her pocket a small address book. It had a dark red cover and was old but showed few signs of age. She'd stolen it from her mother. The little book's condition showed what good care Mary took of her possessions. We are not alike, thought Anna.

She looked under "Kelman" and found Rose's address and telephone number. The same number and street where I am living, of course, thought Anna. She'd examined this "Kelman" page many times before. Now she turned to the back, where there were a few blank pages for notes. These contained a tiny penciled sketch of a llama, and a scribbled statement: "It was the fault of the rain. No, it was my fault. I can't blame the rain."

Anna slipped the notebook back into her pocket and stood up. It would take her an hour to walk home to the rue de l'Alboni.

ON THE BRIDGE the traffic inched forward then came to a complete standstill. If I can crawl across the bridge in the next two minutes, Nicholas told himself, I will not be late. Then he laughed at this lie. He could not arrive on time.

What hope is there of reducing human suffering? We are headed for dark, selfish times, he mused. My work will be of little help. Why don't I relax and enjoy life? Why not emigrate to Montréal? He pictured driving, unimpeded, across the St. Lawrence on the Jacques Cartier Bridge on his way to a tennis game. The Canadians he'd met at symposiums had all assured him they never had to book a court more than a few days in advance. Yes, Montréal. It was quite possible to eat well in Montréal. Montréal was not far from Toronto, where Anna came from. But the serpent was waking, and vehicles were rolling forward. Nicholas grabbed the gear shift and gave it a violent shove.

Five

Eugénie Balashovskaya's fingers tightened around a lump of sheet. She opened her eyes to find herself at home and in her own bedroom. Twenty-four hours had elapsed since her stay overnight at Barbara's.

She turned on her reading lamp and lifted her Bible from the table beside her bed. Why did I tell Barbara to show her work? What sort of man is her Henri?

A brown wool blanket weighed warmly upon her. The white sink with its two brass taps gleamed in a corner of the room. To the left of the windows stood the sombre bulk of her armoire. Eugénie's gaze travelled from the sink to the armoire and back. She could not find what she was looking for. Through her magnifying glass she inspected the words on the open page of her Bible. But what she sought eluded her—an answer to Barbara's troubles. Again she examined the sink and the armoire, then twisted the small knob on her reading lamp, hoping darkness might soften her mind. But her mind grabbed at her conversation with Barbara and shook it.

She saw Rose and Mary on the balcony, talking, seated on folding chairs, suspended above the city. Rose's hair, dark and curly, contrasted sharply with Mary's—white and shocking as snow in spring. Mary's hair startled, created expectations. She was thirty-five years old, four years younger than Rose. Her hair evoked the untouched, the blank canvas, also wisdom and age. Rose did the talking, climbing out of the wreck of her marriage. The movements of Mary's soft hands expressed discreet compassion. Her discerning hazel eyes dissected everything. They seemed to say, "I will not misuse what you tell me, but hold it sacred and intact within me."

Or that is how Rose and Mary appeared to me, thought Eugénie, as I observed them through the glass doors of the living room. Barbara claims I am naïve, that Mary listened quietly and then made cruel use of what she learned. She recalls someone cold and calculating.

The warm blanket pressed down upon Eugénie. She pushed it off. The sheet by its very lightness was suffocating. She managed to free herself from the sheet and climb out of bed. Down the dark, narrow hall she walked, her steps small and careful. She could not remember how it felt to run, only that running had once given her pleasure. Now she found a calmness in moving slowly.

In the kitchen, she took a carton of cream from the refrigerator and from the drawer under the counter the electric beater, a present from Claire and Léon. It did not matter to her that it was the middle of the night. As she aged, day and night grew interchangeable. Perhaps the cool air wafting over her legs, once she had succeeded in tugging the sheet aside, had reminded her of the cream that needed whipping then chilling. The *charlotte russe* must be ready in time for Nicholas and Anna. She'd invited them both to dinner. God moves in mysterious ways, his wonders to perform. The cream thickened around her beaters.

Six

"ONE DAY, LAST YEAR, A BLUE SOFA APPEARED without warning in Mémère's living room," said Nicholas to Anna, serving his grandmother a slice of her *charlotte russe*. This was his favourite of Mémère's desserts, the ladyfingers dipped in Cointreau, holding the Bavarian cream in place. "Someone whose ankles are no thicker than my wrists and who will go unnamed," Nicholas continued, passing Anna her plate, "by superhuman will, dragged a new sofa from her hall into her living room. She did not want to impose upon the delivery men. And why did she buy this enormous blue sofa, in the first place? Because of Mitterrand."

Nicholas enjoyed telling tales, unwrapping them as though he did not know what waited inside, peeling back the layers. He knew he was good at it: the tug of his listener's attention, his own eagerness, the exchange of energies.

Anna dipped her spoon into the *charlotte russe*. When she tipped her head to the right, the room moved with her. She tilted her head to the left, and the room followed. Her glass was again full of dark wine poured by Nicholas's small hand. She wished she knew for certain that he had not seen her run across the Pont Notre-Dame, but as she couldn't ask she took another gulp of wine.

"It was not Monsieur Mitterrand's fault but Aunt Sonya's," Eugénie corrected Nicholas.

"*Ah, bon?*"

"Sonya jumped to conclusions and carried me with her. Although Monsieur Mitterrand is gaining in popularity, he has not yet taken power, nor snatched away our money. Sonya was being hasty."

"Sonya was often wrong, but we all listened to her. If that has been established, may I continue my story, Mémère?" He offered Anna a conspiratorial smile. He reached for his teaspoon and gave it a twirl, so that it spun in circles on its back.

"Of course *mon petit*. Tell us your story."

You're nothing but a boy, thought Anna. You may have left home but you bring your grandmother your laundry to wash. She's told me so.

"*Bon.* An article in *Le Monde* celebrated Mitterrand's growing popularity. The next day Aunt Sonya called to tell Mémère she must run to the bank, remove her savings, and buy something the government couldn't steal from her. So Mémère bought the heaviest sofa in Paris, one even the government would have difficulty loading into a truck. And the election is yet to come. That is all. The tale of how Mitterrand found his way into Mémère's living room." He smoothed his moustache and studied Anna's mouth. Had she enjoyed his story?

"Don't you like my sofa?" asked Eugénie, smiling with satisfaction. So long as Nicholas was seated in front of her, he could announce that he disliked every stick of furniture in her apartment without inflicting the slightest bruise on her soul. He had very nearly not come for dinner. He had phoned to say that if he did not arrive by eight-thirty to give up on him. One of his patients was in the grips of a dark crisis. While Eugénie talked to him on the telephone, the carrots had burned. A caramel odour had twisted along the hall. She had picked out the least charred vegetables and set them aside. If he must call and interrupt her cooking, he must accept imperfect carrots. A few disappointments build character."

"On the contrary, Mémère, your sofa is superb. Very blue, but superb," declared Nicholas.

"Who was Aunt Sonya?" asked Anna.

"Sonya? That's true, you never met her. How foolish of me!" said Nicholas. "She died last year after Mémère bought Mitterrand. Ah, my great-aunt Sonya. She was not truly my great-aunt but Mémère's cousin. She was a tiny woman, ferocious, with the eyes of an eagle. One of the first women in France to be named a judge. She had little hands like claws, covered in rings. No one dared to disobey her. I would've studied music but Sonya wouldn't hear of it. Her brother was one of the finest violinists in Russia before the Revolution. No one in our family was allowed to consider a career in music unless they showed the potential of equalling *l'oncle* Anton. Sonya told me I had no hope of becoming great. She recommended medicine." Nicholas lighted a cigarette. "Would you like one?" he asked Anna.

"No, thank you." Had Eugénie not been there, Anna would have accepted. She would have discovered how a cigarette tasted, and Nicholas could have shown her when to breathe in then out.

Eugénie's eyes closed. Anna, seeing Eugénie's chin drop to her chest, decided that this was her chance, if not to smoke, then to ask a question.

"Why does your sister dislike me?"

"Has she been unkind?" asked Nicholas, alert, setting down his cigarette.

He's prepared to defend me, thought Anna. He believes in knights and jousting matches.

"No, she hasn't been unkind, just cold."

"Her feelings for you, I expect, are ambiguous. She wasn't fond of your mother, whereas I was seduced by your mother's gentleness and beauty. My sister has a jealous nature. After my mother died, my sister didn't want life to move forward..."

Eugénie opened her eyes.

"Were you sleeping, Mémère? Or pretending to?" he asked.

"I was sleeping, I think."

Nicholas rolled his napkin ring along the table. He felt relieved that Friday had come and that Mémère had invited him to dinner, though Anna's question about Barbara had unsettled him. He recalled the rainy days when he and Barbara, as children, had played illicit games of catch in this apartment with its long corridor. In the embrace of this round and familiar room, he felt affirmed. Here, he could not imagine himself as the cheating fiend Janine had painted him to be in the months preceding their divorce. His ex-wife's accusations, however false, had burrowed under his skin. They'd made their home in his flesh, like ticks.

He'd fallen in love with Janine when they were students. He'd climbed the steep marble steps in the inner courtyard of the Hôtel-Dieu, entered the Amphithéâtre Trousseau, and sat through a lecture on disorders of the intestine. He'd held her hand in his, while taking notes with his free hand. Following the lecture they'd descended the white steps together. They'd passed beneath Christ's promise engraved over the arched entrance: *"Qui credit in me etiam si mortuus fuerit vivet."* It had been raining. Janine had raised her small, tidy face and looked up at him. Pigeons cooed in the painted rafters above, undeterred by the shards of glass intended to drive them away. Rivulets of water trickled down Janine's forehead and across her pale cheeks. They'd waited in each other's arms for the rain to stop, while on either side of the courtyard, doctors in white coats scurried down long passages and darted in and out of doorways.

When they divorced, he'd offered Janine their tiny jewel of a house, hidden in the heart of the thirteenth district, surrounded by old working-class cafés and Arab restaurants. She'd refused his offer, preferring cash. Nothing could dissuade her from believing he'd brought women home while she was working late at the hospital. His patients? Why not? In her mind, nothing was beneath him or too absurd. Her heart had become a jungle of lush jealousies, the home of crocodiles.

Nicholas set the silver napkin ring in motion. He observed its progress across the crumb-strewn table cloth. The ring came to a halt in front of the water jug. He retrieved it and sent it on its next journey.

The ugly, middle years of his childhood, he reminded himself, were dealt with. During the long psychoanalysis he'd undergone as part of his training, he'd felt he was gagging on dust. Later he'd drowned in tears, then arrived on land solid enough to call freedom, the best to be hoped for. But on particularly dark, wet mornings, Janine's and Barbara's accusations blended, assaulted him as one, formed a united front with the rain.

ANNA WATCHED NICHOLAS roll his napkin ring over Eugénie's red tablecloth. Again Eugénie's head had fallen forward, her chin sunk into the woollen abundance of her breasts. The silver ring struck the glass bowl containing the *charlotte russe* and came to a stop. Nicholas looked up at Anna, smiled, retrieved his toy and pursued his game.

Anna accepted his long silence as an honour, a sign of the ease he felt in her company. She was witnessing a private act. He might as well have stood up and removed his shirt. She studied the shape of Nicholas's fingers. His entire attention was fixed on his napkin ring. She listened to the ticking clocks, to Eugénie's uneven snoring.

Nicholas had not been blaming Aunt Sonya for his failure to become a musician, Anna decided. Rather, he'd sounded amused. What did he find funny? That he'd ever considered struggling as a pianist, or that he'd allowed his grandmother's cousin to choose his career? But you aren't truly anyone's prisoner, not even Aunt Sonya's, thought Anna. You are like a swallow. She pictured him circling in the evening air, snatching insects, bending a wing, lifting the tips of his elegant tails, wheeling, swooping again, devouring another detail, swallowing another hovering idea from the atmosphere. At night he must return to his nest. Is your nest lined with mud? she wondered.

"How are your classes? Have you made friends?" asked Nicholas, snatching up his napkin ring and setting it aside. "Hugo... Didn't you say that you were taking a course on Victor Hugo? Forgive me for not remembering."

The warmth of his enquiring gaze rippled through her. "Yes, I am taking a course on Hugo. And another on Balzac."

"Whose idea was it, that you come to Paris?"

"Mine."

"Did your mother encourage you?"

"She did and she didn't. She isn't decisive."

"I suppose people told you that Paris is beautiful?"

"Yes."

"And is it?"

"Yes. Very beautiful."

"If you stay a bit longer, you'll tire of it. You must have discovered, by now, that the air stings your throat, and that it rains ceaselessly, without pity."

"If you're tired of it, you could leave."

"Yes, I could." Nicholas laughed and smoothed his moustache. "But I haven't the courage. Don't you feel homesick?" he asked.

"One weekend I went to the countryside and returned to Paris by train. I fell asleep and woke in the Gare du Nord. I'd dreamed I was sitting at home on my front porch, talking with friends. The Gare du Nord looked huge and horrid. I wanted to go back to sleep. But mostly I'm ok."

Eugénie's eyes opened. "Anna has so many friends she hardly knows what to do with them all. She is out every night of the week; and last weekend she had to choose between an invitation to Normandy and another to the Dordogne."

"Is this true?" Nicholas asked, studying Anna's face.

"Absolutely. I have dozens of friends."

"Really?"

"Yes. I do."

"How did you meet them?"

"In cafés, in lecture halls. I go to the theatre, and sometimes I ask whoever is seated beside me to go out for coffee after the performance."

"And do they accept?"

"Some of them."

"I'd never have the courage to do that."

"In a foreign country you might."

"You flatter me."

His gaze leapt to his grandmother. "Mémère, sit. I will clear the dishes. Sit." Once more, his amused eyes examined Anna. "I must take you out for supper one evening to a truly fine restaurant. Yes. I should do that—if you would accept?"

"Perhaps. If you ask me...."

"I will ask you."

"Have you spoken with Barbara?" Eugénie asked Nicholas.

"The only person I know as stubborn as Aunt Sonya is my sister Barbara," replied Nicholas, pushing back his chair and standing. "And now I must clear the table and leave, Mémère. It is long past my bedtime. The next time Barbara drags you across the city in the night to hold her hand, don't tell me about it. Or rather do, but not when I'm at the hospital and not in the hope I'll sympathize with her, or with you for being so foolish as to go." Nicholas bent and kissed his grandmother's cheek.

"It wasn't dark when I left," offered Eugénie.

"Very well, you didn't cross the city in the dark, but you stayed overnight. Did she mention Ivan Sherbatsky?"

"Yes."

"There you are. Nothing has changed. Forgive me, Anna, for again speaking of someone you don't know, or perhaps your mother has mentioned him?"

"No. She's told me nothing. Should she have?"

"That I can't say. But one day I will tell you the story."

Anna wanted to ask, "Will you tell me why my mother

wrote in her address book, 'It was the fault of the rain?' And will you kiss me?"

Nicholas carried the dessert plates in a stack to the kitchen, took his coat from the armoire in the hall, and returned to the dining room.

"As always, Mémère, you prepared a splendid meal. You're an angel. Let me kiss you again. Sit, Mémère. I can see myself out."

But Eugénie stood up, and Anna as well.

Nicholas turned to Anna. "What a pleasure it has been, *ma belle.*" He would have kissed her cheek but she held out her hand. Nicholas, laughing, accepted her choice and called her, "*Ma petite Anglaise.*"

From the doorway Anna and Eugénie watched him wait for the noisy little elevator. It arrived and gobbled him up.

Seven

Two weeks had passed since Mémère's overnight visit, and Henri was still in London. His assignment had been extended. Barbara's concierge had stopped borrowing lemons but he came up, once a day, to ask if there was anything in her apartment that needed repairing. Such behaviour was hardly normal.

All Barbara's mornings at work resembled one another. They began and ended in a room without birdsong or windows. She could not convince herself of their utility. On this particular morning, she opened a letter that lay waiting on her desk and read, "To whom it may concern. The lamp I purchased at your store makes a terrible buzzing noise. I don't know what the damned shade was made of, but it has burned up."

After answering fifteen such letters, she went down the hall for a drink of water. When she returned, Marie of the Perfect Eyebrows at the next desk over was filing her nails. Hurrah, thought Barbara, a nail file! We can saw our way out. But she said nothing. If she spoke, they would expect her to do so again. She mutely answered ten more letters concerning frying pans. Someone had found a sticky lump of chewing gum hidden inside his new teapot.

At last, evening came and set Barbara free. She made her way along crowded sidewalks until she reached the Jardin du Palais Royal. It was tucked behind the Théâtre de la Comédie Française. She passed through the arched entrance and sat beneath a stooped chestnut tree. In front of her unrolled the garden's orderly, rectangular, calm. There was not a person about.

She watched the fountain toss white plumes into the cold air. A miniature brass cannon crouched in the garden's centre. The declaration, "*Horas non numero nisi serenas. Je ne compte que les heures heureuses*" was carved into its side. She hadn't noticed the words until last week. Paris, she thought, is full of lies. The sun was setting.

She got up and walked along the Galerie Montpensier. The plaster ceiling was crumbling. From each arch hung a voluptuous glass lamp. She arrived at Monsieur Mesnil's shop, but he'd lowered the metal grill inside the windows and left for the day. She pressed her face against the glass. The yellow silk dress, from a production of Molière's *Le Médecin malgré lui*, had not been sold, nor had the opera glasses that had once belonged to Marcel Proust's cousin. But the shoes worn by Arleti in a 1940s production of Sartre's *Huis Clos* had disappeared. So Mesnil did part with his treasures now and then. No hats, however. Nothing suitable for *Uncle Vanya*.

Barbara left the garden, entered the Métro, and was crushed among strangers.

HER BOOKS WERE AS LOVELY as ever. Home and safe, Barbara settled on the floor in front of them. On the lowest shelf, the plays pressed against each other. It was Aunt Sonya who had chosen acting for her. "A wardrobe mistress? *Mais voyons.* I can think of nothing more tedious. No. You must stand on the stage, not hide in some back room. You will speak and they will listen. Of course you must not hide. Life demands courage, and in this family we have never lacked bravery."

A slender volume titled *Ubu Roi* protruded. Barbara had not pushed it in properly the last time. She pulled it out.

"Fifteen years ago," she said, holding up the book for Henri to see, though he was not there, "at the age of nineteen, I marched self-important and unforgiving across a stage, a captain of the guard. Did you know that, Henri?"

But Henri was in London. Large, gentle Henri with his misconceived perceptions of her. That he claimed to love her was cause enough for her to doubt him. She squeezed *Ubu Roi* back into its spot on the bookshelf.

"My hair served as a plume, Henri, pulled through an opening in the top of my triangular cardboard hat. You should have seen me, *mon cher*. I was a captain of Ubu's royal guard, Le Capitaine Bordure. The small theatre was filled with the faces of strangers who stared up at me, as though I were the moon. They expected something. I marched with my left eyebrow raised, my lips stretched thin and mocking. I had the power of the tides upon their sleep. I would make this audience speak of me after the show. Crouching as if to look at them more closely, wrapping my long moustache around my finger, I suddenly wished those spectators would all go home and leave me to cry alone. Then I would never have to march for anyone again."

Barbara ran her eyes along the spines of her books until she came to Anouilh's *L'Alouette*. She opened it. The date she had bought the play was inscribed in bright purple ink inside the cover.

"Purple ink, Henri. I used to write in purple ink. Can you believe it?" She held out the open book in case such brilliant ink might be seen all the way from London. "I played another soldier that year, Henri. I was the young Jeanne d'Arc. I burrowed my hand in the thick fur behind my sheepdog's ear. The voice of God told me, '*Jeanne, sois bonne et sage enfant, va souvent a l'église.*' And later, '*Jeanne, va au secours du roi de France et tu lui rendras son royaume.*' That role was easier. There might as well have been no audience. Their coughing, every sound they made was eclipsed by the voice of God in my ear and the warmth of my dog's fur between my fingers. Imagine how powerful I felt, Henri, and at once tiny."

Barbara returned *L'Alouette* to its proper place and got up from the floor. I was right to quit acting, she thought.

I was a fool to have tried. I wasted so much time. The night that I forgot my lines, I walked off the stage and out the back door of the theatre. Anyone else would have stayed on the stage and invented something. But I couldn't. Nothing was true, everyone was acting. "*Va au secours du roi de France et tu lui rendras son royaume*," was fine for Jeanne, but what was I to believe in? Mémère's Right Thinking? Nicholas's gods—Marx and Freud? Didn't anyone but me remember the doors slamming? Was I the only one who knew that everyone was performing?

For dinner, Barbara warmed a bowl of leek and potato soup. She ate seated upon one of the three hard chairs in her green living room, whose colour reminded her of her unpleasant brother.

As soon as I overcome my fear of ladders, she promised herself, as soon as my lecherous concierge gives up, I will paint the entire apartment white.

She ate in the company of her dolls. They watched her chew and swallow with the same sweet interest they showed in everything she did or said. But they were not all sugar. Each of them had absorbed some child's misery a hundred or more years ago. They bore also the marks of their makers. Someone's hand had painted their lips and in Sarah's case had slipped, leaving the corner of her mouth thick. There were three dolls: Sarah, Delphine, and George. George—for George Sand—was made of wood: the other two had porcelain heads, glass eyes that moved, and real hair. George's black hair was painted on.

Her soup bowl empty, Barbara laid the dolls side by side on a folded sheet on the floor. She covered them with a child's wool blanket with a silk border. She'd bought it at the Porte de Clignancourt flea market and had washed it several times by hand then repaired it, using her tiniest stitches.

She took out her sewing basket. For George, she was making a miniature of the dress she'd designed for the professor's wife in *Vanya*. One taffeta sleeve, the dark orange of a tulip, remained to be sewn.

Eight

A MONTH HAD ACCUMULATED then dissolved since Eugénie's birthday party. Henri had not yet returned. Barbara stood on the Métro platform marked "Direction Gare d'Austerlitz" and thought about her grandmother's age. It was cowardly to expect Mémère to continue forever, she decided. Then she noticed the wrist of the woman standing beside her. It was a fragile wrist, pale and delicate. Barbara had never seen such fine bones.

The stranger had pulled back her sleeve to read her watch. She glanced up, and the beauty of her eyes startled Barbara. They were almond-shaped, the irises nearly as black as the pupils. A striated, sparkling black.

The woman acknowledged Barbara with a smile, then paid no further attention to her. Why should she have? Perhaps she was trying to fit the information her watch had given her into the jigsaw puzzle that was her day. She began pacing a brief distance back and forth along the crowded platform. She was reciting something under her breath. Then she stopped her pacing and yawned, half covering her wide mouth with her tiny hand.

Barbara continued to study the woman. Her cheekbones, like two small cliffs, made Barbara think of leaps into the unknown.

The woman yawned again and undid the buttons of her coat. A burgundy coat, soft and elegant. Barbara became aware of the heat. The day was overcast, and people had dressed for the cold. Now many were unfastening their coats. Barbara found herself yawning and covered her own mouth.

Under the pretext of checking for a train, Barbara stepped closer to the platform's edge, where the woman was now standing. The heat was becoming unpleasant. Perhaps the ventilation system wasn't working properly.

The woman had begun reciting again, in a whisper, what sounded like a poem. Her voice resembled an alley sheltered by trees, shadowy and rustling. Barbara recognized enough words to decide the language was Russian. The woman put her hand to her forehead. Barbara saw her sway. Below the lip of the platform, a few feet down, stretched the gleaming rails.

As the train swept into the stifling station, the woman's head fell forward. Barbara grabbed her by the arm and pulled her backwards. The innocent train, with its sealed windows and quiet rubber wheels, shot the length of the platform then stopped, something hissing under its belly.

"I thought you might fall," explained Barbara.

"I could have. Thank you. I was feeling faint. *Quelle horreur.* It's this heat."

People yanked the metal handles, and the doors shot open, air whistling. Passengers burst out of the train onto the platform. A whirring sound, followed by a loud buzzing, warned that the doors were about to close. People crammed themselves into the train, others scurried off along the subterranean corridors. The doors shut and the train became quiet and rolled away, disappearing into the dark tunnel.

On the silent platform stood Barbara and the woman in the burgundy coat.

"Could I buy you a coffee?" Barbara heard herself offer. "I'd like to. And perhaps something to eat?"

"Yes. I should eat. I must. I sometimes don't, which is silly.

That's what made me feel faint, that and the heat. Perhaps there's something wrong with the ventilation?"

"Yes, something is wrong with the air. It's made me thirsty. Shall we find a café?" Barbara was not accustomed to befriending strangers on the Métro. She felt exposed, thrust into the open. Yet she wanted this. She succumbed to the exhilaratingly giddy sensation of taking a risk.

"But of course we must find a café," accepted the woman. "We must at least drink a coffee together. And I will pay. You saved my life."

"Oh, no, I didn't. You would have caught your balance."

"We don't know that. I might have fallen. It's awful to think of. I was foolish not to eat at noon, especially when I haven't been sleeping well. Offering you a coffee is not big enough thanks, but it will be a start." The woman smiled at Barbara. Her large mouth grew wider, and her small feet carried her quickly along the platform, while Barbara hurried to keep up.

THE TWO WOMEN EMERGED from the Métro into the cool, damp air of the Carrefour de l'Odéon.

"The Relais has a non-smoking section at the back. *Ça vous dirait?*" said the woman.

"*Oui. D'accord,*" agreed Barbara.

They skirted the base of the bronze statue of Danton pointing to the sky. His wisdom was engraved below his feet. "*Pour vaincre les ennemies de la patrie il faut de l'audace, de l'audace et encore de l'audace.*" Barbara knew his words by heart. "*Après le pain, l'éducation est la première nécessité du peuple.*"

At the back of the gaudy Relais, they seated themselves on an L-shaped vinyl bench surrounded by mirrors and immense, colourful parrots painted on glass.

"We haven't introduced ourselves. My name is Liuba Zaitsev."

"And I am Barbara Kelman."

The waiter appeared and stared at the toe of his left shoe.

"*Mesdames?*" he enquired, without looking up. They ordered coffees and for Liuba Zaitsev an omelette and a *salade niçoise*.

"On the platform, you were reciting something," said Barbara.

"Yes, that's true. Did you think I was mad? It was a poem by Osip Mandelstam, 'Valkyries Are Flying.'"

"I didn't think you were crazy. On the contrary. I recognized the words 'violins sing' and 'stairs.' But that's all. My Russian is abysmal."

"You speak Russian?"

"I don't speak it. I remember a handful of words."

"But this is remarkable. Don't you think so?" exclaimed Liuba, setting down the piece of bread she'd taken from the basket. "You were translating what I was reciting; you were standing next to me, concentrating on Mandelstam's poem, and then you saved me from falling?" Her hand described in the air the fatal tumble not taken.

"Yes. I suppose. If I did save you. But I could make out only bits of the poem."

"Of course you saved me, you and Mandelstam together." Gratitude emanated from Liuba's black eyes. Barbara's forehead tingled with embarrassment and pleasure. "And my Russian is not splendid either," continued Liuba. "I speak it only with my mother. I should read, but there is so little time. Not time enough to eat. That was very stupid of me, to have skipped lunch. And what was I doing, standing so close to the edge? Did I think I could force the train to come faster?"

Liuba's omelette and salad arrived. Barbara watched her eat. The fragile bones in Liuba's wrist twisted dangerously as she manipulated her fork. There was the heedless breadth of her mouth. Whoever made you, thought Barbara, got carried away when it came to your mouth.

"I'm shocked that you speak Russian," said Liuba, stabbing a section of tomato. "Did you learn it in your family?"

"Yes. What little I learned."

"Were both your parents Russian?"

A frightening desire to tell this woman the story of her life beat inside Barbara's chest, flapped its wings against her rib cage.

"No. My father was French. My mother was born on a ship sailing from Russia to Italy." Barbara described Eugénie's marriage, her departure from Kiev, the death of her husband in America, her return to Paris, and Rose and Claire's French upbringing in the hands of a Russian mother who insisted on speaking to them in English while living in Paris.

"Mémère treats Russian the way a child does a food with a strong smell. It's her broccoli; she'd rather let it grow cold, hide it under her napkin. My brother says it's because Mémère did not like her own mother, who was a cold woman, but adored her Swiss governess. At an early age she discarded her maternal tongue. But my brother is a psychiatrist and believes he knows the answer to everything."

As Liuba listened to Barbara's quick breathing and the fast pace of her words, she heard a beating of wings. A bird is caught in this woman's chest, she thought. An angry, panic-stricken starling. Liuba was accustomed to pressing her ear to people's chests and interpreting the rhythms of their breathing.

"I don't want to bore you with my brother," said Barbara. "He's a pain. Won't you tell me about yourself?"

"As much as you're interested in hearing," answered Liuba. She caught the waiter's eye and ordered a linden tea. Then she began her tale.

"My parents and I emigrated from Moscow when I was two. We settled in Toulouse, where my father opened a pharmacy. My father was a small man who trimmed his beard into the shape of a triangle and listened with concentration to everything I told him. He died when I was twelve, and the number of my mother's good days lessened. She's prone to depression and often lies in bed, drinking tea and reciting poetry. Then she becomes energetic and goes to the theatre three nights in a row. Shall I go on?"

"Please do."

"I live with my mother out of a mixture of duty and love."

Is that an honest way of putting it? wondered Liuba. She did not speak to many people about her mother. "At times it's wonderful living with her and at other times a burden. On her good days she plays the piano and sings. When my father was alive, she gave public recitals and also acted in small roles. He encouraged her, as he did everyone. My own abilities on the piano are rather limited. I'm a doctor, a lung specialist. It was my mother who taught me the importance of breathing."

So, she's a doctor, thought Barbara, and I answer letters of complaint at the Samaritaine. How can she want to have anything to do with me?

As if to confirm Barbara's fears, Liuba glanced at her watch and gasped. "I had no idea of the time. My mother was expecting me half an hour ago. I promised her we would have dinner together as it's Friday. She'll be worrying."

A convenient excuse? wondered Barbara, fishing in her large shoulder bag for her wallet.

"But I am going to pay," said Liuba, setting more than enough money on the table. "You had only a coffee. And you saved me from being crushed by a train."

They stepped out of the café onto the wet pavement, which glistened in the sterile light of the street lamps and they walked down the Rue Dauphine. At the corner, Barbara slipped her arm through Liuba's in an act of wild faith.

"Will you recite 'Valkyries Are Flying'?"

While Liuba recited in Russian, the clouds with their grey cargo of rain pressed down on the roofs of the city.

> Valkyries are flying, the violins sing,
> The bulky opera's finale nears;

Flunkies burdened with heavy furs,
Await their masters on marble stairs.
In the gallery a ninny still applauds;
The curtain is ready to descend.
Cabbies stomp, dancing round bonfires.
"Prince so-and-so's carriage!"
The audience leaves. End.

In Barbara's mind Russian words were surfacing, each one a shard of something broken before her life or her mother's had begun.

Nine

Eugénie sat with her mending, in the greyness of the early afternoon.

"Will you tell me about the Revolution, Mémère, the one you fled from?"

Anna had walked home from the Sorbonne, defying a fine rain. She intended to spend the afternoon reading Balzac, but had made no plans for the evening—not for lack of trying. None of her friends had answered her calls. In her restlessness, she now paced in front of Eugénie, stopping at every plant, staring at a pointed leaf, then a shiny round one, and thinking how much easier than hers a plant's life must be.

Eugénie Balashovskaya, seated beneath blue and orange Kiev, set her sewing aside. She watched young Anna move from leaf to leaf. You're like a bee in a jar, she thought. But if I could lift off the lid, would you know what direction to fly in? How will you find your path? You will, I'm sure of it; you'll not be like Barbara.

"Don't you remember the polka-dotted sheets, Mémère? You said that you and your husband arrived at night in a small town..."

A young man attended the same Hugo lecture as Anna on

Tuesday afternoons. He smelled of cigarettes. His lank, dark bangs hung in front of his deep-set, weary eyes. Several times Anna and this boy had sipped coffee opposite each other, crushed against a round table in a cramped café not far from the lecture hall. The coffee was bitter, and she'd allowed herself to drop in a lump of sugar which fell slowly apart. The young man never seemed in a rush. He was sick of Paris, he told her, and he longed for a beach. "What is there to do on a beach?" she had asked. He said he wanted to lie under the sun, to feel the sun's warmth on his skin. She imagined making love to him. There was a muscle in his arm that she wanted to touch.

Once they sat together in a dark cinema, but he didn't take her hand. The room being full, they sat in the front row. Enormous images appeared on the screen in front of them. Anna didn't care about this young man, what he read or where he lived. She only wanted to feel his lips pressed over her own. She liked the smell of him. But he did not kiss her. She possessed a quality, she was sure, that prevented any man or boy from touching her. What this trait was, she couldn't say, yet she did not doubt its existence.

"Polka-dots?" said Eugénie.

"You told me you saw them on your pillows. The Bolsheviks were advancing."

In Eugénie's thoughts Barbara crouched, her darkness leaving little room for anything else.

"Ah yes," said Eugénie. "The sheets and the pillowcase. We were fleeing the Red Army, my husband and I. We had arrived in a small town after dark, and so my husband accepted a room in the first hotel we came to. In the morning when I woke, what do you think? Beside my head the pillow was covered in tiny black dots. Oh, I said to myself, what curious cloth; and then the dots moved."

"And then?" asked Anna, as if she did not know what followed.

"Well, can you imagine? They were not dots but bedbugs." Eugénie's laugh erupted, loud and complete.

The purpose of Mémère's entire being at this moment, thought Anna, is to release such a laugh. She laughed back then, too, in the grimy hotel. She was so much in love, she didn't care about bedbugs. They amused her. And that was in the middle of a war. That war was real. My life should feel easy, but it doesn't. Who am I fighting?

The pillow and the bedbugs scurrying to hide from the morning sunlight disappeared in Eugénie's imagination behind a curtain of Barbara's black, wiry hair. If only Barbara could find a job that interested her, thought Eugénie. Although Nicholas is a psychiatrist, he has not been able to help Barbara. He does not know how to pray.

"Weren't you scared of the war?" asked Anna.

"No. I was too young and self-absorbed. Only music interested me, then the next week the novels of Dickens. Have you read *Little Dorrit?*"

"No, Mémère. My education is full of potholes."

"*Little Dorrit* was my favourite. I cried and cried."

"Mom says you didn't learn your English in England but in Boston, and that a Boston friend of my grandmother's gave her, that is my mother, a letter of introduction to you."

"Yes. Mrs. Strang. She wrote to me that your mother was lovely, and she was, and I'm sure she still is."

"But who was Mrs. Strang? Without her, I wouldn't be in this living room." Anna had decided that Balzac could wait.

Eugénie laughed. "What a long route to my living room! Mrs. Strang was the wife of Mr. Strang. When my husband and I arrived in Boston in 1920, we started attending the Strangs' meetings. They were both excommunicated Christian Scientists. Half a dozen others attended. Their drawing room had leaded windows that overlooked Coppley Square and the soot-darkened bricks of the public library. And what do you think? The soot was a gift from the train station, the price of speed.

"We spent Tuesday afternoons distracting Rose with a wooden dog on a string, and Claire with the shining buttons of

Volodya's vest, while we listened as well as possible to Mr. Strang's discourse. Little children are demanding, Anna. I have never liked them much." She laughed. "However, they improve with age.

"All other afternoons my husband rehearsed or taught the cello, and I walked Rose and Claire in the public garden. White swan-boats full of idle citizens glided on the water."

Eugénie's gaze fell upon her mending. "How lazy I am. These are Nicholas's underpants. He'll come tomorrow for his laundry, and I won't have it ready," she announced.

Anna forced herself to look away from the white boxer shorts showered with green stars. She got up and walked to the window. Nicholas wore those; they contained him. I will not look at his underpants again. Her imagination wrestled with the image of his penis folded behind the cloth. First she pictured it pointing this way then that. No, she told herself. No, that would be too dangerous. But why? The image vanished from her head. A dizzying vacancy remained. She forced herself to ask another question.

"What does Claire think of the Strangs?" she asked.

"She considers their thinking bizarre, as did Rose. But your mother didn't laugh at the ideas of Mr. Strang. How serious your mother was. I believe she frightened Sherbatsky." Eugénie snipped her thread and put away her needle. The waistband was sewn.

"Who was Ivan Sherbatsky?"

"He was a painter, like your mother. And he also came to me with a letter of introduction. Like your mother, he became a close friend of my daughter Rose. The three of them grew inseparable. Once, we were eating ice cream, and Ivan exclaimed, 'Why this ice cream is as cool as Mary.' " A smile played on Eugénie's lips. Then her eyebrows drew together. She remarked, "That is why Barbara couldn't stand Ivan. In part, that is why. He wasn't always careful with people's feelings. He said whatever came into his head."

"Was my mother cold?"

"But of course not. And Ivan didn't think so either." Fatigue rolled over Eugénie in a heavy wave. "Don't you have work you should be doing, *ma petite* Anna?"

"My work can wait, Mémère. What sort of painter was Ivan Sherbatsky?"

The rain had stopped. On Eugénie's desk sat her Bible and a glass egg that held down her bills. Anna's gaze travelled from the egg back to Mémère. She didn't repeat her question because Mémère's eyes were closed. On the sideboard in the dining room, walnuts, tight in their shells, were piled in the blue and green majolica bowl, a birthday gift to Eugénie from Barbara. Shards of walnut shell lay on the tablecloth. She was eating walnuts alone, thought Anna. Mémère spends most of her time alone.

Anna got up, and Eugénie opened her eyes.

"I must be off. I'm only halfway through Balzac's *Illusions Perdues* and I promised myself I'd finish it this afternoon." Anna kissed Eugénie's powdery, slack cheek. Her bag of books clutched against her chest, she ran down the hall, the shadow of her own sloth pursuing her.

ANNA IS GONE. Now I shall have some peace, thought Eugénie Balashovskaya. She switched on the radio. Schubert's *Death and the Maiden*. She knew the music well, yet each note shocked her. Best of all were the tiny islands of silence. Whoever was playing the violin was doing so with courage and daring. Eugénie closed her eyes and opened her ears.

Ten

ANNA OPENED HER BALZAC AND READ. A web of streets formed in her mind. Their names were familiar. She, Anna, had walked along their sidewalks.

"In Paris anything can happen," cried Lucien de Rubempré. At last, Madame de Bargeton had pulled up in her carriage.

Anna's heart pumped madly. She felt as though her bedroom might at any moment transform itself, flowers bloom from the marble mantelpiece, the faded silk billow free from the walls. There would be a knock at the door. Nicholas.

Anna looked down at the page in front of her. "An idea," she read "can be neutralized only by another idea." Oh, she thought, how true, how splendid, and she had to stand up. How could she sit when such a sentence existed?

Inside the darkness of her own head, ideas began unfolding like ferns, Honoré de Balzac's novel their soil. Thoughts about journalism and the demons of progress.

To quell her excitement, she closed the book, then stuffed the notes she had taken into the drawer of her desk. There lay her father's letter. I'll answer it this evening, she promised herself.

ALTHOUGH ANNA'S FATHER believed that the French took themselves too seriously, he had agreed to pay for her year of study abroad. He'd done so only to please her, for in his opinion novels in any language were not worth tearing apart. If structure interested Anna, he maintained, she would do better to dissect plants. Surely leaves and bark could provide her with all the poetry she required? Anna forgave him his opinions, because he was generous and forthright. She knew where she stood with him. It was her mother whom she had trouble forgiving. Why had Mary stopped painting? "I didn't have it in me. I suppose I had nothing more to say, I didn't know what to paint."

Anna didn't consider this a satisfactory answer. At nineteen she detested excuses and believed in the truth. She often went up to the third floor and examined her mother's old paintings, searching for an answer in the canvasses.

The large, sunny room had been Mary's studio when she first married. But within a year she had given up her vocation. She had an infant to care for. If she went up to her studio while Anna took her nap, she quickly fell asleep on the sofa under the sloping roof, and her brushes remained untouched.

"Was it because of me you stopped?" Anna asked at various ages. But Mary insisted that motherhood was not the cause. She was unusually adamant about this, and Anna chose to believe her. Her question, however, lingered.

"Why did you stop?" asked Anna, yet again, the year before she went to Paris. They were in the kitchen, Anna washing the dinner dishes and Mary drying them.

"I didn't have it in me," Mary answered, out of habit.

"That's not true," retorted Anna. "You did have it in you to paint, and you still do." Her hands covered in dish soap, Anna felt impatient, ineffectual.

That morning, Mary had written to Eugénie Balashovskaya, to explain that her eighteen-year-old daughter, Anna, was determined to study in Paris the following year, and did Eugénie know anyone who rented rooms to students?

Determination, Mary apologized, was one of Anna's principal character traits.

Now, instead of putting away the plate in her hand, Mary stood looking at her daughter. "You needn't shout at me. What gives you the right to tell me what I'm capable of or not? You'd never put up with me speaking to you like that."

"I'm sorry," said Anna. But secretly the fact that her mother was angry, and for once unable to hide it, pleased her. She glanced in her mother's direction. Tears were welling up in Mary's eyes. Anna's sense of triumph vanished, eclipsed by a mixture of remorse and surprise. "I'm sorry," she repeated, this time with conviction.

"You should be," said Mary. Then she hid her face in her hands.

"Mom," said Anna, standing awkwardly beside her mother. "I didn't mean to. I'm sorry."

"I'm being foolish," Mary dried her eyes on the back of her hand. "I'll be fine in a minute. I don't know why I'm so upset."

Mary forced herself to smile.

THE FOLLOWING DAY, Anna asked her mother if she could have a painting to hang in her bedroom—one of Mary's. She often asked why they couldn't hang a few of her mother's canvasses in the living room. Her father would remark, "I used to come across a painting of your mother's in every room of the house, the first year we were married. But then your mother took them all down, and I quite missed them. Or some of them."

"It was time for a change," was Mary's excuse.

To Anna's surprise, however, on this day, Mary agreed to her request. Together they went up to the third floor.

"There are lots to choose from," said Mary, embarrassed. She picked up a paint-stained rag and put it down again, beside the sink where she once cleaned her brushes.

"I know which one I want," announced Anna. She slid the canvas carefully out from those leaning against it.

"The chess players?" Mary asked, startled.

"Yes," said Anna, wondering if it was her choice or the painting itself that was responsible for the expression of mild alarm on Mary's face.

The two women in the painting had no faces. That was partly why Anna liked it. A game of chess was unfolding on the board between them. They looked mysterious. And the colours were rich, each stroke vigorous.

"Don't you like this one?" Anna asked.

"I do. As a matter of fact, it's one of my favourites."

Anna waited, but as Mary said nothing more she asked, "Did you paint it in Paris?"

"Yes. Just before I left."

"Can I have it? Or borrow it, that is."

"You're welcome to hang it in your room. But I'm not sure it's one I'm prepared to part with..."

"You don't have to give it to me." Of course she doesn't have to give it to me, thought Anna. Whenever Mom has to refuse me anything, it makes her nervous. She wishes she lived in a world without conflict.

"I know I don't have to." Mary felt stupidly anxious, and eager to return downstairs. "I'm glad you chose that one. I'm very fond of it. And it's the right size for your room."

ANNA FILLED A POT with water for tea. While the kettle heated, she tugged open the drawer of the chest where she stored the mismatched china Mémère had loaned her. The chest had been intended for clothes, and its drawers were deep and difficult to manoeuvre. Anna found a cup and saucer. A weak sun seeped through the thin curtains covering the tall doors at the end of the room. Anna yanked the doors open, then carried a chair onto the wet balcony. She brought out the teapot with its chipped lid, milk in a glass, the cup and saucer.

The thick wall that ran the length of the balcony came

higher than her waist. She peered over it and down. No one was in the narrow street below. The line of parked cars appeared permanent. It was hard to imagine that in such a treeless street, grey and lined by tall grey buildings, anything ever moved.

Anna buttoned her cardigan against the cold air. She pulled Mary's red address book from her pocket and turned once more to the pages at the back. "It was the fault of the rain." What part of herself did Mary say goodbye to when she left Paris? Anna wondered.

The week before at the Musée Rodin Anna had walked in a circle around a white, marble head of a young woman. Two supple hands of stone formed a loose cage in front of the young woman's open mouth. A small brass plate gave the statue's name—*L'Adieu*. Who was the young woman saying goodbye to? Was she the one who was leaving, and if so, why? Anna had felt, gazing at the statue, that this girl of stone was telling her something urgent about light and air, desire and impossibility, the spaces between her fingers. Then Anna had turned and seen *La Convalescente*. Another woman's head. This one was sinking, illness and the weight of her hair pulling her back into the marble slab from which she'd struggled free. Again, hands raised to a mouth. The forehead's beauty and clarity on the point of being stolen by pain. Next, Anna had discovered a cluster of tiny, jealous, green, onyx women huddled on benches, gossiping in a two-walled room. A gathering of witches. By the time Anna had reached the second floor, and Balzac laughing in his dressing-gown, she could not concentrate. She'd escaped to the garden, wandered between dark tree trunks in the freshness of the winter air.

Two days later Anna had written to her mother to tell her all she'd experienced at the museum. Mary had replied:

> Ah, the Musée Rodin. His sculptures are my
> favourites, and isn't the museum itself lovely, full of
> light from the garden? I had tea there once, with Rose

in a café under the trees. That was the time she told me her husband was having an affair. Should I be telling you this? You already know that her husband left her. I'm sure I've told you that? And now you're in Paris, who knows what you're learning? A great deal, I expect and hope. I want you to enjoy everything. Anyway, as I've begun I may as well continue.

    We went and stood among the bronze statues of one of the burghers of Calais. In the first sculpture the burgher had his clothes on; in the next he had them off. Once he had arms and once he was without. Rose described the François Kelman she'd fallen in love with—the lean, studious father of her children—and the François Kelman who was sharing a bed with an American woman in Germany, six months of the year. They were the same man, and that was dreadful. She was trying to stop loving him. But how could she? She convinced me, without intending to, that the loneliness I lived in was a small price to pay for my freedom.

Anna had found her mother's sudden openness delightful yet perplexing. What does she believe I'm learning? Anna wondered. She also wondered how anyone could will themself to stop loving someone. To do so would involve building a dam, redirecting the flow of one's blood.

    Anna had picked up Mary's letter and continued to read.

But I didn't intend to tell you about unhappy things. I adored the Musée Rodin and often went there to draw. I'd go on weekday mornings, early, before the crowds. It didn't matter that his statues were cast in metal; they were alive. The *Thinker* was concentrating so hard, he was holding on with his toes, all but the large one on his left foot. That one toe was gripping nothing. Rodin made stone flow. Do you agree? I think he was fascinated by water, the sea. So often, hair forms heavy waves. I remember the wings of Icarus's sister becoming a wall of water and collapsing over her, sweeping her under. Rodin saw life as tossed into the brine, submerged, thrust up again. But I'm probably not expressing myself well. And I'm sure you don't want to dwell on my experiences of Paris, but to go out and live your own. The zoo was a lovely place to draw. The llamas had poise. That is all of my Paris I will burden you with for now.

Mary had never spoken to Anna about art, or about anything else with such passion and insight. Anna had folded the letter carefully and put it away.

Now, standing in her narrow balcony, she turned the pages of the stolen address book. The pencilled sketch of a llama's head stared at her. Who steals from whom? she wondered. Are mothers or daughters the greater thieves?

Neither understanding her own question nor able to provide an answer, Anna lifted her teacup and emptied its cold contents over the wall into the street below. She gathered her tea things and retreated into the warm apartment.

BEFORE COMING TO PARIS, Anna had asked Mary, "Did you have a lover when you lived there?" She didn't like to risk angering or shocking her mother, not when she was leaving in two days, but she wouldn't have another chance to ask. And she needed to know. She'd convinced herself she had the right to ask.

Several folded shirts lay stacked on her bed. Her open knapsack lay on the floor. Above her dresser hung her mother's incredible painting.

"Yes. Very briefly." answered Mary. Then she added. "Hardly at all."

"What was his name?"

"His name?"

"Yes," insisted Anna. But suddenly she felt tired of always pushing. Why am I so heartless? she wondered. She wanted to stop packing, to sit and cry. "Will it be cold there?" she asked. "In Paris."

"More raw than cold. I'd pack several sweaters," said Mary.

SHE WAS USING the same bar of white soap to clean her teacup that she'd used in the shower that morning. She hated spending money on boring things like dish detergent when there were so many films and plays to see. I'll go out on my own tonight, since no one's free, she decided.

She returned to the faded silk walls of her bedroom and sat down at her desk. But instead of taking out her notes on Balzac, she pulled from the drawer a cheap journal with a green cover.

She wrote:

> In the black and white snapshot, Mary Bertram is standing on Madame Balashovskaya's living room balcony, her waist tiny. The Eiffel Tower soars behind her, unhesitating. A grey sweater covers her small breasts. Her eyes disclose everything and nothing, a mixture of pain and hope she appears to be telling you, calmly, are all in your imagination and have nothing to do with her.

Anna read this last paragraph and felt pleased. She continued.

> The day the photo was taken Mary Bertram had bathed by dipping a sponge in a basin of warm water while crouching in the shivering air of her studio. The large room with its high ceiling and immense

windows swallowed the efforts of the kerosene heater in a single gulp.

Anna set down her pen. She could not re-examine the photo, which was stuffed into a shoe box in Mary's bedroom at home in Toronto. But the basin of water and sponge were true. Mary had described them, on the day Eugénie's letter arrived, offering Anna a bedroom and tiny kitchen of her own.

"I took a sponge bath every day. I couldn't afford to heat the studio, not adequately," said Mary. She was unpacking groceries, fitting them into the kitchen cupboards and the refrigerator.

"How did you keep warm?" asked Anna, plugging in the kettle.

"I wore layers of sweaters and got used to the chill."

"Tell me something else."

"The size of the studio was splendid, and I was lucky to have it. It belonged to Mémère's cousin, Madame Sonya Grêle. According to some law passed at the end of the war, if Aunt Sonya had left the studio empty, the government could have put anyone in it and required that they pay her next to nothing in rent. The law had been passed when all sorts of displaced people were searching for homes. Aunt Sonya wanted to save the apartment for a wealthy friend who was considering purchasing it upon her return from abroad. To keep it occupied and under her control, she agreed that I might live there."

"What about Mémère's apartment?"

"I never lived there. It was full. There was Rose, her children and sometimes her husband, and, of course, Mémère. But they were generous, and I visited often. I'd find the air stifling, since I'd taken to wearing so many layers of clothing.

"My second winter, Rose, the children and Mémère left for a two-week holiday. I think they went to Nice and stayed with friends. They asked me to look after the apartment. I took slow baths in their big tub. The bathroom was painted a gorgeous dark blue. When you go there in September, you can tell me if the bathroom is still the same shade of blue. I hope it is."

"Why did you come back to Canada? Couldn't you have stayed?"

"Forever?"

"Why not?"

"My grant money had run out. It was only meant to support me a year but I'd stayed on a second. My father had given me a bit of money and I babysat and tutored some children in English. But it wasn't enough. I couldn't go on like that. I was thirty-six years old and my paintings weren't selling."

"When did Rose die?"

"The summer I left. Just before I was to leave."

ANNA LOOKED DOWN at her notebook and picked up her pen.

Mary walked. She walked for pleasure and because she had only a little money. Several of her paintings had been shown in an exhibit of works by young Canadians, organized by the Canadian consulate, but none of hers had sold. She walked to Madame Balashovskaya's under a clear sky, through cool autumn sunlight, hurrying so as not to be late for lunch. To arrive late would have wounded her own pride and possibly spoiled Madame Balashovskaya's cooking.

What had they eaten for lunch? As Anna couldn't decide, she skipped the meal.

After lunch, the taste of coffee drunk black from a small cup lingered in Mary's mouth. Madame Balashovskaya opened the doors to the grey balcony. A breeze carried up the noises of the city. "Let me take your picture," said Rose from the doorway. Rose pushed a wiry black curl from her forehead then lifted her camera to her eye. "Maman, will you stand a little closer to Mary, please? Good."

The photo taken, Rose lowered the black box and with her naked eye studied her Canadian friend who had neither husband nor children, a woman intended for solitude. Rose wondered for what she herself was intended. "And now Mary on her own." Once more she lifted the black box to her eye.

Mary did not look into the camera's lens but past it. She did not smile, afraid to disturb the serenity of her face. To smile would be false. She refused to have the camera record a lie.

Anna read what she had written. I've got part of it right, she decided. It wasn't only her beauty that prevented Mary from smiling. Something else was turning like a screw inside her. Ivan Sherbatsky?

Anna closed her notebook. She flopped on her bed. Why do I bother? What does it matter who she was? If I were cleverer, I'd capture her easily. My brain is sloppy. She pictured Nicholas's brain, sharp and shiny, hanging above her, its infinitesimal cogs perfectly chiselled. She lay on her back gazing up at the gleaming workings of his mind, and a peacefulness filled her, as though she were complete.

IT SEEMED TO ANNA she'd spent a lazy hour resting on her bed, but her watch told her only fifteen minutes had elapsed. She remembered she'd bought nothing to cook for her supper. It was past four. She leapt up and took her coat from behind the green curtain. She dropped her journal and wallet into her shoulder bag, then opened her bedroom door.

In the sitting room, the radio was playing. Behind the glass doors slumped Eugénie in the embrace of her Mitterrand. Her knitting lay on the floor. Her head had dropped to her chest. The man on the radio talked on.

Anna opened the apartment door then pulled it shut behind her, making as small a bang as possible.

FIRST SHE RODE on the Métro, then she walked. She could have bought her vegetables close to home, but in the rue de Passy nothing unusual was likely to happen. She got off near the Sorbonne and made her way to the market, rue de Seine. There were people her age walking in every direction, but she knew none of them.

The vegetables were piled in mounds. The grocer wore a bright blue apron, wrapped over his ample chest and stomach. She chose him because the fullness of his moustache gave her an absurd confidence in his vegetables.

"Two courgettes, please."

"Only two?" he asked, grinning at her.

"Yes. I don't eat much."

He weighed her courgettes and fitted them into a small paper bag, their ends sticking out.

"But you must eat more, or how will you make love?"

"I don't know," she said, blushing. "Thank you." The wind blew a strand of her hair across her face and she brushed it aside. "Thank you," she repeated.

She walked down to the Seine and started on her long walk back to the rue Alboni, accompanied by the blue of the grocer's apron and his full moustache, wriggling, a furry animal beneath his nose, riding his grin. To him, it had seemed not only possible but natural that she might make love to a man. Next to her, below the wall, flowed the river.

AS ANNA FITTED her key into the lock, she heard a man's voice.

"*Ah, bonjour,*" said Nicholas, delighted, walking up to her and kissing her on either cheek. "You've arrived at the perfect moment."

Eugénie, kneeling on the floor in front of her hall cabinet, was rummaging in a cardboard box.

"*Voilà*. What do you think?" said Eugénie, holding an old snapshot close to her eyes.

"If you'll let me have a look, I'll tell you what I think," replied Nicholas.

As Eugénie handed him the photograph, she explained to Anna, "It is a photo of your mother. Nicholas came to collect his clean laundry, though he'd said he wouldn't come until tomorrow, and, *heureusement,* I'd done his mending. He asked if I had an old snapshot of your mother. He remembered seeing one long ago. He insisted I must have it somewhere."

"What do I think?" said Nicholas, passing the photo to Anna. "She's every bit as beautiful as I remember her. No wonder I fell in love with her." His eyes rested upon Anna. He smiled. No, he thought, you do not resemble your mother. Your eyebrows haven't the elegance of hers, but perhaps your mouth is prettier. The shape of your face and your eyes must be your father's.

"Have you seen this photo before?" he asked. "Does your mother have a copy? I was eleven years old when I met your mother and fell under her influence. It was a fall. Love always is. Don't you agree?"

"I don't know. I've never fallen in love."

"Ah."

Anna stared at Mary's slender waist, the soft sweater concealing her small breasts. There was the balcony railing, preventing Mary from tumbling down into Paris. The iron determination and grace of the Eiffel tower climbing behind her neat shoulders. Her mother's gentle mouth and questioning eyes. Yes, it was the same snapshot, with white scalloped edges, that she'd tried to describe in her journal, a few hours ago; that she'd wished she could examine.

Eugénie gripped the door of the cabinet and pulled herself up from the floor, the ninety-year weight of her life tugging her downwards. Nicholas offered his hand.

"Thank you, *mon petit*. Do you recognize this one?" She handed him her second find. "This one is of me and of Mary. We had taken the train to Pouligny then walked to Arcelon, as one did in those days. One weekend, Anna, I will invite you to my little house at Arcelon, if Nicholas will accept to drive us. That time I went with your mother alone. Rose couldn't accompany us, because Nicholas and Barbara were in school, and she had to work. It was a weekday. By the time we arrived I was too tired to run a bath. After dinner I went straight to bed without washing. In the morning the weather was fine, so Mary and I breakfasted in the garden. Then I looked at my feet beneath the table. Well, what do you think I saw? My toes were black and my calves coated in brown dust from the road. I wished the ground would open and swallow me, along with my shame."

"What did my mother do?" asked Anna.

"She said she had not washed her feet either, and we laughed so hard our ribs ached. Later I told Ivan Sherbatsky of our little adventure, mine and Mary's. He said that Mary had beautiful feet, and I asked if he planned to paint them. He promised me that if Mary would permit him to do so, he would make me a drawing of her feet. I must have the drawing somewhere. I will look." Her cane leaned against the wall. She grasped it and, setting her sights on her bedroom, began her journey.

"You'll look for the drawing another day," said Nicholas, catching her, turning her about, leading her back to the nearest chair. "I must be going. And you have had enough rummaging for one day."

"You promised you'd tell me a story about Ivan," Anna said to Nicholas.

"Yes, I promised the other evening, didn't I?"

"Yes. You like making promises."

"*Ah bon?* And don't you think I keep them?"

"I can't tell yet."

"In general I do what I say I will do. I try to keep my word. Sherbatsky, in brief, was an artist, a family acquaintance who became my mother's lover after my parents' divorce." He turned to his grandmother, bent down, and kissed her. "And now I must be off. I'm late."

As soon as he was gone, Anna cut her courgettes into slices. Tiny hairs grew from the sturdy stems, of which a stub remained.

Eleven

ONE SMALL TABLE WITH TWO UNOCCUPIED CHAIRS. Barbara stuck her head into the tiny room, spotted the two seats, and claimed them. On Fridays, customers—many of them students and professors—crammed themselves into the Patisserie Viennoise as though it were a departing ship. The week over, they were all eager to set sail. The café served thick hot chocolate and layered pastries named after forests, symphonies, and generals. These were displayed on delicate metal trays in the front window overlooking the narrow rue de l'École de Médecine. The walls of the small back room where Barbara waited for Liuba were a rich egg-custard colour, then sank into a dirt-concealing burgundy wood panelling. Seven tables, a bench, and eleven chairs had been squeezed into the room. Barbara counted eight people besides herself. The steamy hiss of the coffee machine, the thick china knockings, and the quick clatter of spoons scattered the various conversations, and everyone pecked with their ears at crumbs of each other's lives.

Liuba squeezed past the counter and poked her head into the back room.

"You didn't forget," exclaimed Barbara, standing up. "I thought you might. I'm glad you've come."

They kissed each other on either cheek.

"I'm sorry to be late. Someone stopped me with a question just as I was leaving."

Barbara had made a grave decision.

"I have something to show you." Anxiety moistened the palms of her hands. From beneath the table she pulled her folder of drawings and untied the black ribbons.

She placed the drawings in front of Liuba. In the first one, Astrov wore a straw hat and was seated in a garden at the outset of Chekhov's *Uncle Vanya*. On a separate paper stood young Sonya, heartbroken in a pink dress sprinkled with forget-me-nots.

"The brim of Astrov's hat used to be wider, but I made it smaller and stuck a feather behind the ribbon. It seemed important that something stand up in his hat, possibly as a sign of his pride—the pride of the isolated," Barbara explained, drying her damp palms on a paper napkin. Then she hid her hands in her lap and filled her lungs with air.

Liuba examined the sketches, holding them with caution. When the waitress appeared, Liuba ordered a pot of tea and Barbara a hot chocolate.

Liuba set the drawings down and twisted the ring on her finger. Then a broad smile relaxed her face.

"That dark red shirt suits Astrov. He could wear it riding through the forests he's planted. There was still a flame burning inside him, wasn't there?"

"Yes." How did you know why I chose that colour? thought Barbara. It was a miracle, a small one. Liuba had agreed that the red of Astrov's shirt was perfect. She hadn't suggested that Barbara show her drawings to the world. Instead she'd studied them and understood. An intoxicating gratitude beat inside Barbara's chest.

"Won't you tell me about your week?" suggested Liuba. She handed Barbara the drawings. "Thank you for showing me these. They are excellent."

"*Merci.* No. You go first."

"Mine was horrid," Liuba began. "I botched my piano lesson since I hadn't practised."

Barbara did not believe this. She felt certain Liuba failed at nothing.

"And your work?"

"I have three new patients," Liuba continued, "all of them teenagers who are destroying their lungs. I've suggested they quit smoking. They think I'm telling them to stop having sex." She stood up. "I am going to choose a pastry. Will you have one?"

The pretty pastries sat in the window, their names inscribed on paper tags held above them by slender metal poles.

Liuba chose a *napoleon*, and Barbara a *symphonie à l'Amande*. They carried their indulgences back to their table.

"I hope your week was not as horrible as mine?" concluded Liuba, piercing her pastry with her fork.

"There's something I may as well tell you. In about three months' time, I am going to be married."

"Congratulations."

"His name is Henri. My family doesn't believe I will ever marry."

"What's he like?"

"Henri? He wears turtlenecks and hunts rabbits. He rows in a skiff with other men. He's heavy but tall. And he enjoys putting on a suit and going off to keep order among his employees. I'm not in love with him. Or perhaps I am."

"You don't give the impression that you are."

"He has no idea who I am. He simplifies me. Whatever I say, he mashes it until it's smooth, like something you'd serve to an infant. Then he raises the spoon to my lips. He's often away. When he's gone, I get scared he won't come back." Barbara pulled the drawing of Sonya out of her folder, shoved her plate and cup aside, and chose a blue pencil. "Do you mind if I draw?"

"Why would I mind?"

Barbara drew a row of tiny buttons down the front of Sonya's dress. She hadn't thought she could bring herself to draw in front of anyone. Now she knew she could. She felt exhilarated.

"What do you think? Should the buttons continue all the way to the ground?" she asked.

"Yes, do add more buttons," Liuba agreed. "And could we think of an excuse for Sonya to wear a hat? She might be carrying one."

"I don't see why not. I'd have to check the text to be sure."

"May I borrow a pencil? Orange, if possible. And a sheet of paper?"

Barbara found a clean sheet of paper and made room for her pencils between the teapot and the hot chocolate.

The two women sketched and sipped in silence.

"There, I've done it," said Liuba, admiring the lavish, inappropriate headgear she'd just created. "What do you think? Is the plume too much? I haven't drawn anything in years. I have a weakness for birds and hats." She returned the orange pencil to its spot.

"It's not for Sonya. But it would suit the professor's wife," said Barbara.

"Would it?" Luiba asked.

"Yes."

"Why don't I get tickets? Someone must be doing Chekhov."

"I might spoil your evening. I'm very particular."

"I'm sure you wouldn't. I'll see if anyone's performing *Uncle Vanya*."

"Hats," said Barbara, gathering up her pencils, returning her drawings to the safety of their folder. "My mother drowned, trying to catch her hat. That's what my brother claims. But he's wrong. She wanted to fall in. How many people climb on the railing of the Pont d'Austerlitz for no apparent reason? She was already up there when her hat blew off."

It's not sympathy she wants, thought Liuba, and she stopped herself from offering any.

"What were your mother's reasons for wanting to drown herself?"

"My father's swinishness. A young Russian painter who smelled of pickles. Another painter, a Canadian, spending time abroad. Her name is Mary, and now her daughter is renting a room from my grandmother. Everyone adored Mary. My brother followed her around, his eyes even more sober than usual and his hands nervous. She and my mother talked endlessly, and I was jealous. Then my mother died. I was fourteen and Nicholas twelve."

"What went wrong between your mother and this woman Mary?"

"Mary slept with my mother's lover, Ivan Sherbatsky. I'm the only one who seems to care. Mary painted a portrait of my mother. It hung in my grandmother's dining room. I was the only one who couldn't stand looking at it. Finally Nicholas took it. I'm sure he still has it."

"What happened to Sherbatsky?"

"He left Paris. He used to write to my grandmother from New York. Then he stopped writing. With any luck he's dead."

Liuba looked at her watch and frowned. "I'm so sorry. I'm afraid I must go at once. I promised my mother I'd be home an hour ago, and that I would stop at the Comedie Française to collect her scarf. She forgot it there last week." Liuba took her coat from the hook on the wall.

"Could I offer you a ride? They're holding the scarf. I'd be only a minute at the theatre and then I could drop you off. If you're going home."

"But I live near the Canal Saint Martin."

"I'd enjoy your company. This visit has been so short. We've hardly spoken."

"Yes, I'd like a ride. Thank you."

As Barbara tied the ribbons of her folder, she felt she was

packing all her worldly possessions and embarking on an uncertain journey. She thought, with an ache, of her dolls, of George's painted black shoes pointing at the ceiling, her wooden cheeks that had brushed against roses, and her prim mouth.

They walked to the car.

"Will you recite something?"

Liuba recited Mikhail Lermontov's "When the Yellow Rye Field."

When the yellow rye field billows in the breezes
And the fresh wood answers to the wind's low thrum,
And deep in the orchard, hiding in the shadow
of a cool green leaf, hangs the purpling plum;
. . .
Then repose is granted to my troubled spirit,
Then no more with wrinkled brow I mope and plod,
And I can conceive of happiness on earth here,
And I can believe that in Heaven I see God.

AS THEY DROVE, rain clouds piled behind the rooftops. The traffic advanced in spurts. By the time Liuba found a parking spot near the theatre, the first cold drops were falling. At the box office Liuba collected her mother's scarf.

"And now," she said to Barbara, "I have something to show you."

They stepped into the shelter of the Galerie Montpensier and walked beneath its high, crumbling ceiling.

"There. Look." Liuba stopped walking. In the window of Monsieur Mesnil's store hung an orange silk hat.

Barbara stared at the hat. Surprise, fear, and delight battled inside her.

"Do you know this shop?" Liuba was asking.

"I come here all the time," said Barbara. She stared at the

hat. Emptiness hides behind the things I love most, she thought. She could feel Liuba's enquiring, black eyes fixed upon her.

"Then you've seen the hat?" asked Liuba.

"No. It wasn't here the last time I looked."

"It's the one I tried to draw, the one you said would suit the professor's wife. Except I added a few more feathers."

"Yes, I recognize it."

"I like this shop. I find small presents for my mother, old musical scores, a pair of gloves, a scarf. But Monsieur Mesnil is rather odd. He won't always sell what he puts on display."

"I don't mind him. I don't try to buy anything. I just look. He lets me take my time." Barbara imagined running down the long gallery and into the wet garden, past the fountain made ridiculous by the rain. She knows everything about me, this woman in the burgundy coat. She comes to Mesnil's shop. She's a stranger and I've told her everything.

But Barbara didn't run. She stayed put. Choose. Choose not to run, Mémère would say.

"Couldn't we go in?" Barbara heard herself ask. "You could call your mother and tell her where you are, if Monsieur Mesnil would let you use his phone."

"Yes. Let's go in."

There were no customers in the shop. Monsieur Mesnil looked up from the rose-coloured shoe in his hand. He was sewing on a button.

"Good evening, Monsieur Mesnil," Liuba said. "What awful weather we are having this winter!"

"The weather is changeable. People do not change. We are all fixed in our ways."

"I wondered if I might use your telephone, just long enough to call my mother. She was expecting me some time ago."

"Of course, Madame. Mothers are important." He gestured towards the telephone on his desk.

In moments, all was settled. Madame Zaitsev told Liuba that she would practise the piano until Liuba got home. The rain had improved her spirits, and she had cooked a pot of soup. She was preparing a piece by Mozart.

"This rainy weather cheers her. She feels she belongs," explained Liuba. "In sunny weather she believes it's her duty to feel happy, and she fails. That's as close as I come to understanding it." She turned her ring round and round on her finger.

Barbara picked up the orange hat.

"Theatre du Nord. 1948. Summer production of *Uncle Vanya*," Barbara read aloud from the paper tag pinned inside the hat. Again, delight, fear, and surprise battled inside her breast.

Liuba came over and looked at the tag.

"Incredible."

"You didn't know?" asked Barbara.

"I only saw it through the window. Its colour caught my eye. When you showed me your drawings, I remembered it."

"I don't know who wore it," said Monseiur Mesnil. "The theatre's records might name the actress, if you cared to know." His hands were clasped behind his back, his bald head tilted to one side, too heavy for his thin neck. He walked slowly back to his desk.

Barbara lifted the veil and ran her finger along the velvet trim. The orange silk flowed into gold and plummeted into depths of red.

"I'd like to buy the hat for you," said Liuba.

"I can't accept." Barbara set down her treasure.

"But why not?"

"Because I want to give it to you. Please accept. You drew it. It's yours. And I want to give you something." Barbara picked up the hat and held it out.

"Then you'll have to give me something else. I'm the one who's indebted to you. And I don't want this hat. Or not nearly as much as I want you to have it." Liuba lifted the hat from Barbara's hands and made her way between the bird cages, cloaks, and sceptres.

"Monsieur, I should like to purchase this hat for my friend."

Monsieur Mesnil pulled his thimble from his finger, and with a shrug of his thin shoulders he accepted. From behind a stuffed parrot he produced a hat box.

And so the orange silk hat, worn by a forgotten actress in a 1948 production of *Uncle Vanya* became the property of Barbara Kelman. Though Barbara had succumbed to Liuba's greater will, she did not feel diminished. She walked in a state of excitement along the Galerie Montpensier, her hat box dangling from her hand. In the street, Liuba raised her lemon yellow umbrella and the two friends walked beneath it to the safety of Liuba's car.

In la rue de la Grange des Belles, Liuba pulled over to the curb. Barbara glared through the car window at the dark green doors of the building where she lived. She did not want to go home.

"My concierge knocks at my door and asks to borrow things," she explained, "unless Henri is over. When Henri is about, he vanishes. Sometimes he waits for me on the stairs. He smiles his feeble smile and watches me unlock my door."

"How unpleasant. Are you safe?"

"I think so. In any case, I'm not moving." Barbara opened the car door. "Would you like to come up?"

"My poor mother is waiting."

"Of course. I forgot. How stupid of me." Barbara felt jealousy rising inside her. She pushed it down. Mémère is right. I must not let weeds choke the garden. She got out of the car and, holding her hat box, watched Liuba drive away.

Twelve

Anna woke in the middle of the night, one thought on her mind: she owned nothing pretty to wear on her feet. This thought had chased her up through the pool of her sleep until she broke its surface. What will I wear if Nicholas does take me to an elegant restaurant?

The metal shutters, pulled tight on the inside of the tall windows, shut out the city's lights. She'd grown accustomed to the steady roar that pressed against the glass at all hours. She reached over and switched on the lamp. On either side of her windows, pink and white candy-striped curtains hung to the floor. Had Rose chosen them? Had Rose and François used the small kitchen, where she now cooked and showered, as their dressing room?

Now that she was awake, Anna felt hungry. She opened her door and walked past Eugénie's bedroom to the main kitchen. Bread crusts hung in a cloth sack behind the door. Apricot jam filled jars. On the highest shelf, above the windows, plums floated in vinegar.

Standing on the tips of her toes on top of Eugénie's kitchen stool, Anna took what she was after. She reached with a spoon into the tall glass jar and fished a plum from its vinegar bath.

She chewed the stolen fruit, removing its pit with her tongue. As she balanced on her island of wood in the darkness of the kitchen, she listened for footsteps. But Eugénie did not come and catch her.

Two Persian carpets lay where the hall widened. Anna crossed them. She passed the broad doors, bolted for the night, and entered the living room. There stood Nicholas's piano. Everything in this night apartment belonged to his small hands, to the dark hairs growing from his wrists.

She opened the tall doors and stepped onto the cold balcony. Directly in front of her, across the river, stood the Eiffel Tower. It had been wrapped and filled for the night with orange light. She preferred it when it climbed naked and solitary during the day. A tower that winds and birds explored.

The chill of early March slipped through her nightgown, making her shiver. She retreated indoors.

From behind the table supporting Mémère's jungle of plants and her stray books, the boy in the picture on the mantelpiece examined Anna with sober, unhappy eyes.

Can I comfort you, or is it too late? wondered Anna.

Thirteen

"Come in," said Rose. Nicholas opened the door of his mother's bedroom. She and Mary Bertram were seated in front of the windows.

"Miss Bertram, could I ask you to explain? I don't understand English grammar. It's all exceptions."

He laid his book open in front of Mary and stood next to her, his young passion grabbing at the rules of the English language. Mary explained. As she did so, she looked into his eyes to be sure she was making clear the nature of dangling gerunds. When she'd done, her smile caressed him. He thanked her, took his grammar book and went back to his room.

Her son gone, Rose turned to her friend.

"I worry about Nicholas. Look at the treatment he's received from his father. I know it's not my fault. But all the same I ask myself, if I were not so large-boned, so solid, if I were blonde?"

"Don't say that. Please," exclaimed Mary. "You're beautiful. If he can't see how lovely you are, then he's blind."

In Rose's smile happiness and disbelief mixed. She ate a slice of apple.

"François will have to look after himself," she said. "At least he's finally made his choice. If he'd done so sooner, it would have been easier for the children. Barbara doesn't make friends at school. She draws but refuses to show me her work. When she does bring me something she's sewn or drawn, my response is wrong. I'm too critical or too forgiving. Yesterday she told me she's auditioned for a part in the school play. But she wouldn't say anything more, not even the name of the play. She doesn't look where she's walking and bumps into things. She yawns all day." Rose stood up. A sparrow was hopping along the thick grey wall. She opened the doors and put out a slice of apple.

"I don't think Barbara's fond of me," said Mary. She looked at her hands in her lap and wondered how she could have said something so childish. Her hands seemed soft and lumpish.

"Why do you say that?" asked Rose.

"I don't know. I have the impression I make her uncomfortable."

"I don't think she approves of anyone." Rose closed the balcony doors. "She's fond of Mémère. Nicholas she adores and detests. She's critical of everyone and mostly of herself. She sees my suffering and I see hers. We fall into each other's pain."

"Thirteen is a difficult age," offered Mary.

"That's what Maman reminds me. She has invited a young Russian painter to lunch tomorrow. She asked me to tell you that she'd be delighted if you'd join us. His name is Ivan Sherbatsky. Maman says he paints animals in bold colours and spends hours at the zoo. To get by, he washes dishes at a restaurant. He appeared at the door a few weeks ago with a letter of introduction from Maman's cousin, Zalman, who teaches in Moscow. I wasn't in."

"I wouldn't have the courage to live like that, washing dishes in a restaurant."

"Are you sure? I think you would."

"No. I don't have that sort of strength. He'll probably think I'm a fraud. I'm not sure I want to meet him."

"Do come. Maman will be disappointed if you don't. She's only met him once, but she says he has a sense of humour."

"Please tell your mother that I'll come. Thank you." Mary stood up. "Right now I should be going."

"You won't stay for supper?"

"No. Thank you. Not tonight."

"And when shall I come and sit for you?"

"Next week? Saturday morning, if there's enough light."

"*Bon*," agreed Rose. She accompanied Mary down the corridor into the wider hall.

"It was very generous of your mother to ask me to paint your portrait," said Mary.

"She did it because she wanted to. I'm curious to see what you'll turn me into."

"You may be disappointed."

"I don't think so."

Rose stood in the doorway and waited for the noisy little elevator to come for her friend.

FOR THE REST OF THAT AFTERNOON, in his bedroom, Nicholas felt satisfied with himself and with life, convinced he'd accomplished an act of courage in asking Mary to help him with his English grammar. But by evening he was again swimming in awkward longing. He was called to dinner and came to the table, exhausted, as if he'd crossed an ocean.

Fourteen

ALL MORNING, ANNA WORKED ON HER ESSAY, "Balzac and the Demons of Progress." Her ideas—liquid, vapour, never solid—refused to hold still. She floundered, frightened of form, grasping at details. After lunch, discouraged, she put away her essay and pulled out her notebook.

> Paris, January, 1958. Mary Bertram had invited her friend Rose Kelman to dinner. Though the corkscrew was surely in the drawer, Mary could not find it. She left her studio and went down into the street. Five o'clock, and already the street lamps had come on. Orderly winter. Days trimmed to the quick. Days clipped any shorter would bleed. The street lamps cast an untrustworthy light. Prostitutes stood at every corner along the boulevard de Clichy. So long as she walked with a sense of purpose, she felt safe.

Anna frowned and returned her notebook to its drawer. She filled a pot with water for tea and watched the red heat pour from the burner. She went into her bedroom. A letter lay on her desk. It had arrived yesterday.

I'll read this again and answer it, then I'll put on my coat and go to the Centre Pompidou and look at some paintings. That will take care of the afternoon, she decided. She pulled the handwritten pages from the envelope.

Dearest Anna,

Forgive me. I am a terrible correspondent. All week I have had long conversations with you in my head, but not picked up my pen until this evening. Eight days have slipped away since I received your letter. You sound happy. I feel twinges of jealousy as I read your descriptions of the city, of the rosy late afternoon light that bathes the buildings along the Seine, your glimpse of a forbidden courtyard before the heavy blue door swings shut. I remember discovering courtyards that were perhaps similar, and windows with perfect proportions.

We have little news. Winter has decided to stay. The day before yesterday it snowed. The snow has piled three feet thick in the front yard. Then, yesterday the large sailboat Mr. Blackmore has been working on, the one that's filled his yard for the past two years, slipped off its stand and crashed through the hedge into the Clarkes' frozen garden. I suppose that constitutes news. The boat and hedge have suffered, but relations between the Clarkes and Blackmores appear intact. This will all sound very odd to you. News from far away.

Your father has installed a new seat on the toilet and I'm sure he will tell you about it in his next letter. He said the old seat "nipped" him, so he decided to "invest" in a new one. I have been receiving regular bulletins from upstairs concerning his progress. How a bolt rolled across the bathroom floor and he had to hunt for it on all fours until he located it under the corner of the bathmat. The new seat, he reports, does not seem as firm as the old one.

I have accomplished even less with my time, though I've enjoyed this listless day. As you know, we've allowed so many *New Yorker* magazines to accumulate in the porch that the room can now be used for little else. They provide insulation against the weather, your father says. No doubt you would throw most of them out, Anna. You are more ruthless than I am. I mean that as a compliment. You are, I believe, determined in a good way. Do you see much of Mémère? Do the two of you have long conversations, on are you too busy with friends and work? Does she speak often of Rose? . . .

Anna remembered the tea and ran to her small kitchen. A last bubble of water lay hissing in the bottom of the pot. She swore. "*Merde, putain, connard.*" The foul words filled her mouth with a hard sweetness, like almonds coated in pink sugar. These were not words she would have used at home, and they made her feel powerful. She filled the empty tortured pot with fresh water, turned on the burner and returned to her chair.

In the front hall, a door slammed shut. Anna put down Mary's letter. Floorboards creaked. A man's voice greeted Eugénie. Anna got up and positioned herself behind her closed door.

The quick, energetic voice belonged to Nicholas. Two sets of feet, one shuffling, the other precise, approached as close as Eugénie's kitchen. Anna waited.

She sat down on her bed, then got up again.

This time the feet were his, rapid, walking to the living room.

Notes drifted down the corridor and under her door. Carefully arranged, they softened the air, then sent out a shudder, rose and fell in looping patterns.

Now Eugénie was crossing the front hall, pushing her squeaking trolley that she'd nicknamed the Cadillac.

"Ah. You are too kind," exclaimed Nicholas.

So, Mémère must have baked him something, not just brought out the aged bar of chocolate she kept especially for him in her kitchen cupboard. Perhaps it was a tart and they would not eat all of it.

"Won't you play to the end of the piece for me?" asked Eugénie. Anna fabricated these words. But it was almost certainly what Eugénie had asked, for he resumed his playing.

The notes streamed down the hall, no longer made of air but of water. A brook, they flowed under her door. Brahms? She longed to bathe his feet in the rush of notes, to hold his heels in her hands.

Fifteen

THE NOTES ENDED. NICHOLAS TOOK A DEEP BREATH. Had he rushed the melody? Had he done justice to the last phrase? He wanted to tackle another piece but he didn't have time. Besides, the coffee was cooling.

"Thank you, *mon petit*. You played quite well," said Eugénie. "Not as smoothly as last time, but your tone was delightful. Will you play another piece?"

"No, Mémère. Not today."

"Then I will pour us some coffee and cut you a slice of cake. I need a cup of coffee as I am tired."

"Haven't you been sleeping well?"

"Not well."

"Why not?"

"Barbara is not happy."

"Ah, yes. Barbara." Nicholas got up and inspected the trolley. "How could you, Mémère?" He grinned. "Crumb cake."

"It's American."

"I know it's American. So you tell me, every time you make it. That's the trouble with it." He carried the thin flat cake to the table and stared down at it.

"If you expect me to serve this, I propose you provide me with a saw." He smiled at her. "What do you put in it?"

"Bread crusts, a little flour, one egg, a little sugar, and some oil. I like this cake because it uses up my crusts."

"Give them to the birds." He succeeded in hacking off a wedge, which he placed on her plate.

"This recipe is from the *Fannie Farmer Cookbook*." Eugénie pressed her hands with satisfaction, palms down, on the tablecloth.

"Let Fannie eat crumb cake," declared Nicholas. With his fork he orchestrated Fannie Farmer's arrival in Paris, wearing a flowered hat.

"I bought the *Fannie Farmer Cookbook* in Boston. In Boston, in America. It is a Boston cake."

"Ah, why didn't you say so, Mémère? If it is from Boston you're forgiven. I'll forgive you anything from Boston."

"But why?"

"If you don't know, then I won't forgive you."

"Barbara says you will not forgive her."

"Forgive her what?"

"She did not say what."

"You see how impossible she is?" declared Nicholas. "I will eat your Boston cake, because it was in Boston that you were in love." He bit, chewed, swallowed. He watched Mémère consume, little by little, the slice of tasteless America that lay on her plate. It was Tuesday, three in the afternoon, and he should not have come. He could be seeing patients. No matter how he arranged his time, his reading always fell behind, the journals accumulated.

Mémère fell asleep, and he watched her sleep. His beloved, snoring monument. Every few minutes she snorted, not unlike a horse.

He took a sip of coffee, and unfurled Mémère's chronology:

IN 1919 EUGÉNIE SHESTOV, having attained the age of twenty-nine, and fallen in love with Volodya Balashovsky, refuses to leave Kiev. Her parents prepare to depart for Paris without her. "I will not leave," she tells them. I won't go," and the horror of her disobedience spreads through her, as dye bleeds into cloth, colouring every thread.

The fighting has not yet reached Kiev, so she will wait. She can't marry Volodya Balashovsky before his Moscow wife has divorced him, and she will not escape without him.

The Bolsheviks, who are not waiting for a divorce, advance southward. At last, Eugénie acknowledges their existence and marries a married man. Through the intervention of her uncle, the couple obtain passage on a boat bound for Italy. A daughter, Rose, is born to them en route. From Italy they travel to the New World and settle in Boston. Volodya and his cello support the young family. Eugénie bears a second daughter. They name their American infant Claire.

In 1924, the summer Rose is to turn four, Eugénie voyages with her daughters to Paris. For the first time, the sisters meet their grandparents. Eugénie's father spreads open his arms. The sticky buds of leaves burst open on the chestnut trees by the Seine. Shoots poke through the soft earth in the beds of the Tuileries Gardens. Eugénie's mother pours the hot tea and frowns.

It is a hot August for Paris. Word comes by telegram that Volodya is dead. Eugénie books her passage to Boston and, taking her daughters with her, returns to the city where she last saw her husband.

In Boston, Eugénie must support herself. She secures a position as a French teacher at a girls' boarding school. She detests her work and is dismissed at the end of the year, informed of her inadequacies as a disciplinarian.

Eugénie packs her *Fannie Farmer Cookbook*, the children's American school texts, the address of the American Church of Paris, and leaves Boston forever.

MÉMÈRE'S LOWER LIP TWITCHED but she did not open her eyes. Nicholas looked at his watch. In one hour's time, he told himself, my patient Monsieur Carpaud will arrive outside my office and light a cigarette, convinced my absence is his punishment, the outcome of a careful plan. We will spend three sessions establishing that I was held up in traffic. We will examine the meaning, for Monsieur Carpaud, of my failure to arrive on time. There are no short cuts. Someday, I want to arrive somewhere quickly.

Nicholas got up from his chair. A young telephone operator had come to see him at the hospital that morning. "I'm not allowed to hang up," she'd said, "until the client has put down, or slammed down the receiver. No matter what is said to me, I must wait. The client must be the first to hang up. I am not permitted to answer the telephone by saying 'Good morning' or 'Hello.' I must say 'Number 965, I'm listening.' The supervisor can listen in at any time. My responses are timed. If I take too long, I am penalized. But I must not answer too quickly. When I go down the stairs into the Métro I hold the railing. I never used to do that. I only dare cross the street at the lights. At home I answer the telephone, '965, I'm listening.'"

Nicholas pushed the Cadillac over the Persian carpet. The carpet's knots had cost someone their eyesight. Why, he wondered, do I spend so much of my time thinking about human suffering? Because it is everywhere, and increasing. He parked the Cadillac in the kitchen.

It was Josette the conceirge's job to clean the apartment. But years of thoughtless work had dulled her as well. He was curious about the tops of the cupboards. He climbed Mémère's stepladder. What he'd imagined proved to be true. A sticky grime coated the top of the cupboard. With the tip of his finger he wrote Eugénie. The letters unwound through the grime, an ancient stream between soft banks of greasy dust. Eugénie, the name of an empress. He climbed down. In the hall he retrieved his coat from the armoire.

When he looked back into the dining room, Eugénie had opened her eyes.

"Will you have a cognac?" she asked.

"No, Mémère. I have my coat on. I must go."

"One little cognac, in your coat?"

"No, thank you, Mémère. I am already late. The traffic will be terrible. Did you have a good rest?"

"Did I sleep? Then I must have rested."

"What will you do after I go? I hope you will leave the dishes for Josette?"

"Yes." She peered at the face of her watch, lifting her wrist close to her nose. "In ten minutes the Percussionistes de Strasbourg are playing on the radio. I've promised to listen to them."

"Whom did you promise?"

"Barbara told me to listen to them. They have collected their instruments from all over the world, and with these strange instruments they make a lot of noise. But Barbara says they are very clever."

"She's right. They are very clever. She was right to tell you to listen to them. And now I must go." He kissed his grandmother's slack, powdered cheek. Her perfume smelled soothingly familiar.

"A month ago you promised Anna that you would take her out to dinner," said Eugénie, frowning. "Are you going to keep your promise?"

"Yes, I know, Mémère. And are you jealous? Or do you just want me to be honourable, true to my word? This is the second time you have reminded me."

"Am I jealous?"

"Yes, you are as green as one of your plants. But I will treat you to dinner also, on a separate occasion. Now, I am going to leave."

"When you treat me to dinner, I'd like you to take me to the château where we once stopped on the way home from Arcelon, and we ate glazed duck."

"Agreed, Mémère. Together we will eat *canard a l'orange*. But I can't promise when."

Inside the descending elevator, Nicholas thought about Mémère's fragile ankles. Next, he pictured her stepladder. Seated naked on the top of the ladder, Anna bit into one of Mémère's marinated plums. The dark juice ran down her chin and trickled between her small breasts.

The image startled him. Despite the rivulets of dark juice, Anna retained her look of purity. He leaned forward to lick the juice from between her breasts, but the elevator had reached the ground floor. He opened the door and stepped out.

Sixteen

"Will you show me, part way through? Or must I wait until the end?"

"You may look, when there's something to see."

"And I mustn't speak while you're working?"

"It will help if you keep as still as you can. But a few words won't hurt, especially at the start."

"*Bon.* How shall I sit?"

"Face me. Yes. Turn a little more. That's fine. Thank you. Yes, that's good."

THE SMELL OF TURPENTINE was everywhere. I like the smell but I mustn't say so, thought Rose.

The rain lashed the long windows. The kerosene heater was battling the greed of the cold room.

"What did you think of Ivan Sherbatsky?" asked Rose. "There, I've spoken. I didn't last five minutes. It is the excitement of doing something new."

"That's all right. I'm still blocking in your figure. I'm not looking at the details of your face. Not yet . . . Ivan Sherbatsky? He's energetic. I expect he has a great deal of courage." Mary set down her brush. "I haven't got much bravery. He can't turn around and go home. And his father isn't helping him." She studied the marks she'd made on the canvas. "Mémère shouldn't be paying for this. It may not look like you at all."

"I think it will look like me," said Rose. "I'm very curious to see it."

Mary picked up her brush, mixed more umber into the white. Now she saw what she'd been searching for in the shape of Rose's head. She worked quickly, not wanting to lose the essence. With each stroke Rose's head, her shoulders, gained in weight, made their claim. That meant the empty space, the open possibilities shrank. Is that it? she thought. Have I caught her? Yes, the shoulders are hers and the tension in her neck. Later I'll add softness. Will I be able to fill in the rest? Will she be alive?

A painter should enjoy the smell of paint, thought Mary. I don't care one way or the other about the smell. The colours wake me out of this horrible sleep they all want me to accept. The monotony they tell me I should tolerate, at home. The dullness for which I should feel gratitude. But I am grateful for colour. How many times did Ivan Sherbatsky say "structure" during lunch? Twice, I think. That was enough. I won't invite him to see my work. Not yet. He would consider it unstructured, indulgent. It was polite of him to ask. Perhaps not only polite. I expect he adores the smell of paint. A painter should. Could I bear not to paint? When Ivan Sherbatsky looks at his canvasses and hates them, he can't let go of the branch and fall into the rosy clouds of maternity. He can't lie to himself, "A baby would do," and let go.

Rivers of rain coursed down the panes of glass.

"There isn't enough light today," said Mary and she put her brush down again. "I thought this light might do, but it's horrible. Light is essential. I should have waited for a brighter day. But I can't keep asking you to change your plans."

"But of course you may ask. I can sit for you another day. Are we stopping?"

"I don't know. It's my fault. I'm not concentrating. I've got your left ear all wrong. I could make us some tea."

"Shouldn't you go on? I'm curious to see what you've done. Could you leave my ear for later? This horrid rain."

"You're right. I'll go on. There may not be a bright day for weeks." Mary squeezed out more viridian. She saw exactly where the tiniest dab of viridian must go. The certainty of it held her dangling for a moment, above the foggy world, saved. Then she thought again of Ivan Sherbatsky.

"Should we go sometime and see Ivan Sherbatsky's work? He did ask us. We could go together?" suggested Rose. "There. Now I won't say another word. I promise."

"Perhaps. Yes, we could go and see his work."

Seventeen

Barbara waited for Liuba on a green metal chair in the Jardin du Luxembourg. She shifted her position, and the chair's legs made a threatening sound as they scraped against loose stones.

Between the trunks of the trees hid the queens of France carved in white stone. I can't stand it any more, Barbara said, to herself and to the queens. I won't answer any more letters about broken toasters. I won't.

The grace of the stone stairs, the harmony of the long *allées* under the trees, the sailboats becalmed in the fountain's pool—such peace made her heart beat faster than ever. She stood up and walked back and forth, the sun's warmth falling on her shoulders.

Liuba arrived, out of breath.

"Thank you for waiting." In her hands she held two *chaussons de pommes* wrapped in white paper. "I brought these for us. I'm remembering to eat. No more fainting."

"I'm glad you've come. Thank you for the pastry." She kicked at a piece of gravel. "I loathe my job."

"Could you give notice and find something else?" Liuba dropped into the nearest chair and pulled off her shoes. She stuck her legs out in front of her and wriggled her toes. "What warmth for April! Even if it lasts only this one day, it's wonderful. Barbara, you have too many abilities to stay at the Samaritiaine. Don't you think so?"

"The Samaritaine sucks the meaning out of everything. It's devouring me."

"Then you must quit. The price of staying is too high."

Barbara sat down in the chair next to Liuba's. "Are you in love?" she asked without warning.

She'd been waiting for weeks for Liuba to tell her some small thing about her most intimate life. But Liuba had offered nothing, and Barbara was tired of waiting. I am always excluded, she thought.

"Yes. I'm in love."

"What's his name? Who is he?"

"Joseph. But that doesn't matter. I'm in love with him because I've put an end to it. It's over, and so our first days have sprung back to life in my mind. I trip over our happiness in the bathroom, on the street. I feel bruised all over. But we weren't happy." Liuba pulled her shoes on and stood up. "I'd like to walk a bit."

They descended the stone stairs.

Aren't you going to tell me who he is? If you trusted me, if I meant anything to you at all, you'd tell me who he is, Barbara thought.

They passed in front of the fountain, climbed back up to the other side of the park. The harmony of these paths, these carefully pruned trees under this chance blue sky mean nothing, thought Barbara. You aren't going to tell, are you? She bit her lip and went to stand beside one of the queens of France. I can believe in Liuba or not believe, she decided. I could stand here stiff and proud for centuries, while pigeons perch on my head, but she wouldn't tell. What I want most to know I can't find out by walking back to her, nor by staying under these trees. But if I go over, at least I'll be with her.

"Shall we go and watch the chess players?" suggested Liuba, as Barbara reappeared beside her.

"Yes."

The chess players were gathered alongside the card players under the roof. They'd brought little clocks and set up their boards on the seats of the chairs. At the edges of their taut silence exploded the card players' ironic twitters and grumbling concessions. Pigeons pecked at the ground.

"I'm sorry I stormed off," said Barbara. "I have certain questions that will never be answered. I hate that."

"Yes. I know the feeling. You must decide on an answer all the same, and not care who disagrees."

They walked away from the chess and card players and followed the wide dusty path.

"Maman was careful never to stay overnight at Sherbatsky's," said Barbara, "but towards the end it was obvious when she'd been to meet him. She would laugh for no reason and water the plants over and over, drowning them. When she hadn't seen him, she answered the phone as though her life depended on it. In the evenings, while Nicholas and I were doing our homework, she would appear and stare at us, pick things up—our clothes or books—put them down and leave the room. She couldn't sit still and read. I shouted at her once, 'Why don't you go to him, if he's the person you'd rather be with instead of us!' Then my mother stayed still and quiet. 'Perhaps he doesn't want me to be with him,' she said. Nicholas glared at me and asked, 'How can you be so cruel?' I started to cry and he slammed his book shut and said he could get no peace and how was he expected to pass his exams? Did she forgive me? For the rest of that evening I refused to speak to her or to anyone."

They'd arrived at the fountain's pool. A duck was struggling to board one of the sailboats, sinking the vessel's stern. Great white clouds came scudding across the sky.

"He was like that duck, my brother. Determined to sink me," said Barbara.

"You must escape the Samaritaine," said Liuba.

Eighteen

THE FINE WARMTH DID NOT LAST. By Saturday a cold rain was beating spring back underground. Liuba telephoned Barbara to say she could not come to help paint the apartment after all; that she'd been detained at the hospital during the week; that in ten days' time she must present a paper on asthma; that the paper was not yet written. Barbara stared at the green walls of her apartment and then escaped to Eugénie's.

"MÉMÈRE, WON'T YOU TAKE another biscuit? I brought them for you." Rain pelted the windows. Barbara crossed the room and pressed her forehead against the cool glass. "The Seine is pockmarked. I love a storm," she said.

"Do you?" asked Eugénie, and lifted a biscuit from the plate on the coffee table. Such a long way down to a coffee table, she thought. God has mischievously lowered the floor of the room.

"I'd like to be the earth," replied Barbara. "And to feel the water pummel me, reach deep inside me. Wouldn't that be splendid, Mémère? Just think." She crouched beside her grandmother. "Don't you think so?"

"Such a strong rain batters the plants in my garden at Arcelon."

"You're no fun. What's bothering you today?"

"When you are the earth and rain pummels you, do you dissolve into what is largest, into God?" asked Eugénie.

Barbara left her grandmother's side. "Don't talk to me about God. I don't want to know anything about Him."

"I should have remembered, *ma petite*. We will talk about something else. Your dress is lovely. I have not seen it before."

"Yes," answered Barbara. "It's new, and I'm delighted you like it, but there are other things, Mémère, besides God and a dress." She lifted the glass egg from her grandmother's desk and glanced at the paper beneath it. "Your heating bill is monstrously high."

Next Saturday, she wondered, will Liuba help me paint? If I don't call her, will I ever hear from her again? Yes, she is my friend. I will get out the ladder tomorrow and start on my own.

"I have discussed my heating bill with Claire and Léon," said Mémère. "They say there is nothing to be done."

"You have Anna. You shouldn't but you do. I expect she doesn't pay you much?"

"Not a great deal. I don't ask her for a large sum. She's a student."

"Is she a good tenant?"

"For the most part. But she talks a great deal. And there are times I would prefer not to be talked to. Once she left a chair on the balcony. It was raining, like today."

Barbara set down Mémère's glass egg, and at once her hands felt weightless. "That's the sort of thing I do, leave something valuable out in the rain. And I lose things. Was the chair ruined?"

All the umbrellas of Barbara's life, those she'd left on buses or suspended from shop counters now sailed through her memory, proof of her unworthiness.

"No. The chair was fine because I found it in time," answered Eugénie. "I am glad to have Anna's company and to help Mary Bertram with her daughter." Eugénie smoothed the purple folds of her skirt. "Do you like my new skirt, *ma petite*?"

"How can you say 'Mary Bertram' so easily," Barbara exclaimed, "as though it were the name of a hand cream! You are determined to adore her. You know she slept with Sherbatsky and you don't care."

"It was none of my business," said Eugénie.

"None of your business? How can you? You drive me crazy." Eugénie's eyebrows drew together. Her hands were clasped in her lap and she scowled at them.

"She came into my room," said Barbara. "I found her looking through my things, examining my drawings. 'These are quite nice,' she said, as though she had my permission to be in my room. Maman had sent her to find me. But that didn't give her the right to walk in when I wasn't there. She'd opened my door without permission and walked in. 'These are quite nice. You should take lessons.' What right did she have to tell me what to do?" Barbara saw the worry in Eugénie's eyes. I've made matters worse, she thought, that's what I do. My goal, my only talent, is to cause pain. Barbara clenched her teeth and stopped herself from crying. "You see, Mémère, how petty I am? My God, sometimes I think Nicholas is right—I am sick, I have invented it all. Am I the only one who saw?" Barbara crossed the room. She stared through the window, her back turned, every person who had ever breathed within that living room thrown behind her, smashed in a heap.

Eugénie forced herself up from the settee and followed her granddaughter across the carpet.

"I did see. I saw quite clearly." Eugénie kept a polite distance between herself and Rose's no-longer little girl.

"What did you see?"

"One evening your father threatened to kill himself. He said that if your mother divorced him, he would take his life. He began to rummage in the closet. Your mother had turned her back on him and was gazing out the window. I had been brushing my teeth when I heard them shouting. I could not remember if I had turned out the light in the kitchen. To check the kitchen, I had to pass their room, and the door was open. Your father told me to come in. In his lap lay my cousin Misha's old pistol. 'There are no bullets,' your father said. What sadness. I had not heard sadness in his voice in a long time. Anger, yes, fear and sweetness. It was then we heard sobbing. You were lying in your bed in the next room. Your mother ran past me into the hall. I told your father I'd long ago thrown away Misha's bullets and that he should give me the gun. He allowed me to take it from his lap."

Barbara pictured her father's sadness gliding out of him and across the room, a shadow. It displaced nothing. None of her father's emotions were real. "May I see the gun?" asked Barbara.

"In the end I gave it to the police. It is gone."

"I wish he had killed himself. Instead he went on, oozing self-pity and ordering us about, until he got bored and left." Barbara ate a tasteless cookie. "I detest him."

"There are moments, *ma petite*, when I have hated him also."

"Really?"

"When I hate your father, I read from the Bible."

Barbara filled her cup with cold coffee. The Bible. Forgiveness.

"Henri has not come back. I told you he wouldn't." Barbara said.

Eugénie frowned. "Why didn't you say something? How has he been delayed? Tell me," she urged.

"There is nothing to tell. They have asked him to stay on yet another two weeks." Barbara returned to the windows. She pressed her forehead against the cool glass. "The Seine is still pockmarked. If I were twenty, I would open these doors and stand in the rain. Soon I will turn thirty-five. Do you realize that, Mémère? Thirty-five."

"I had not thought of it."

"I am getting old, Mémère."

"Age is in the heart. Do not make yourself old, *ma petite*."

"You, Mémère, will never be old." Barbara crossed the room and kissed her grandmother's cheek. "Thank you, Mémère. And now I must go. I never intended to stay more than an hour. You deserve better. A granddaughter who comes often, and for hour upon hour. Life is cruel and horrid."

"Won't you try one of my figs before you go?"

"No, Mémère."

"They are delicious, a present from Claire."

Barbara again pressed her lips to her grandmother's cheek. Eugénie's fingers gripped Barbara's upper arm. "Will you call me when you are safely home?" she asked.

Barbara pulled herself free. "Of course I'll call. I always do."

A key turned in the lock. The large door swung inwards and open.

"Anna," said Eugénie.

"Hello," said Anna.

"I will get you each a fig," declared Mémère. "You will see how good they are. It is Claire who offered them to me." Eugénie set off to find sweetness hidden in a golden tin.

"What a cold, wet day," said Anna. She looked down at her feet. How ugly my shoes are, she thought. I am not French. I can't help that. Not all Canadians dress as awkwardly as I do.

"Your mother betrayed mine," said Barbara. "She had an affair with my mother's lover. I saw him touch her neck. She'd bent down to adjust her shoe. I saw him touch her." There. She'd said it all in one breath, and now she must leave, before Mémère returned. She opened the apartment door. "Please, tell my grandmother I don't want a fig."

"Did Barbara leave?" asked Mémère, returning, bearing the golden tin.

"Yes. She said she had to go."

"Will you have a fig, Anna?"

Nineteen

"Mary Bertram's beauty eclipsed the walls of buildings, yet it could seep through a crack. It spread everywhere, changed the texture of objects in a room."

Anna stopped writing. "*Merde,*" she whispered. Then louder: "*Merde, merde.*" She jabbed the paper, stabbed the words with her pen.

Twenty

Brakes whistled. The rubber wheels of the train slowed, then stopped. Tolbiac station. Anna flipped up the shiny metal handle and the doors flew open. She stepped out, hurried along the platform, up a flight of stairs, and emerged into sunlight on the broad sidewalk of the boulevard d'Italie.

A map of the neighbourhood was mounted on a pole. Someone wanted to know, "*Pour qui la liberté?*" and had written this question in red ink across the map. Anna located part of Nicholas's street. The rest was concealed beneath the unanswerable question. She walked in what she hoped was the proper direction.

Will I meet you by chance on the sidewalk in front of your house?

Her steps quickened. She reached into her pocket and her fingers touched the hard surface of Mary's address book.

What will I ask you? Is Barbara right? Did my mother sleep with Sherbatsky? In a few minutes, I am going to see the house you come home to at night. Who do you share your bed with? Will you be in bed with someone on Tuesday in the middle of the afternoon?

Anna pictured Nicholas's dark head nestled in his pillow.

His smooth, exposed forehead. The fullness of his moustache. She could not decide on a colour for his pillowcase. She walked faster. She entered his narrow, treeless street, lined with low, drab buildings.

Here it was. This was his house. A smooth beige square punctured by three windows and a brown door. Was he at home?

Nicholas had told her that the house had once been a working-class café. A metal blind was lowered in the large window on the ground floor, where once old men had sat at round tables, smoking and drinking. One of the upstairs windows had been left open.

Would he have gone out and left a window open? A white lace curtain was billowing, invisible fingers of air teasing the delicate cloth. The white paint on the window's frame was peeling. Good, she thought. He can live with imperfection.

She scanned the length of the sidewalk. The street offered nowhere to hide. The minutes were adding up. If he opened his door, what could she say to him?

She walked away, a single and unfounded thought dancing in her mind: If you loved me, you would have been home and found me.

ON THE BOULEVARD D'ITALIE'S broad sidewalk, plenty of people were going about their business. Here and there, windows had been boarded over, following a fire. The arsonist's work completed, renovations could now take place and the rent be raised. It was Léon, Claire's husband, who had explained this to her, who had wanted her to understand that capitalism was ruthless. At a fruit stall, melons were on special. Anna remembered the two plates she'd seen through Josette the concierge's kitchen window. The first plate asked, "How are men like melons?" The answer was painted on the second plate: "To find a good one, you must finger many."

The people in films who took off their clothes and rubbed against each other, in bliss or fury, did not answer any of her questions. She had seen diagrams of men's penises, slack then swollen with purpose. Penises pointing the way. What means did she possess of giving direction? Would she be allowed to finger any part of Nicholas? She opened her wallet while the owner of the stall selected a melon for her. She counted out her money. I will share it with Mémère and I will also bring her flowers. For once, I will have something to offer her.

She looked about for an entrance to the Métro. Beneath the elegant metal arch, grubby stairs led underground. She descended the stairs two at a time. In the tiled subterranean corridor, a man was selling cut flowers from green plastic buckets. Men and women were hurrying past advertisements for new cars and holidays in Corsica.

Anna chose a bouquet of rich red and blue anemones.

Twenty-One

Eugénie Balashovskaya turned on the radio. Resting her head against Mitterrand's blue softness, she closed her eyes. The notes of a cello were parting the air.

Eugénie knew how Volodya had died. His heart had stopped. That much she knew. But was he sitting or standing? How frightened had he felt? Was he facing a wall? Did he think of her? A ring of fog surrounded Volodya's death, cutting off its peak. At best, she could reassemble the day the news had arrived in Paris that he was no longer alive. Her father had taken Claire and Rose to the Bois de Boulogne on that Sunday afternoon.

The girls had enjoyed themselves. She heard the chattering of their high voices, first muffled in the hall outside, then clear and piercing when their grandfather unlocked the door and threw it open. They were two and four years old.

The click of the lock, the sudden noise of human life, shut Eugénie in, did not wake and free her from the telegram she held in her hand. That slip of paper made her a prisoner of a living room that no longer made sense. Why a chair? Who would want to sit in the middle of loss? Why a table?

When they—Rose, Claire, and their grandfather—entered the living room she did not speak, but handed the telegram to her father.

"Maman?" asked Rose.

"*Ma petite* Eugénie," her father said quietly, "*ma chère fille.*" His thick arms held her against his chest. She listened to the beating of his heart. For a moment his solid hand rested on her shoulder. Then he released her, saying to the children, "Your mother asked me to purchase some milk and I forgot. Come girls, we must go and get some milk for your mother."

"I don't want to," protested Claire, her eyes fixed upon her mother.

"Come. I think we might also find you an ice cream."

"I want Maman to have an ice cream, too." Claire dropped her grandfather's hand and ran to her mother.

Eugénie crouched to let Claire between her legs and into her arms. But she could not speak. Her eyes went to the doorway, to meet Rose's eyes, filled with the same frightened comprehension as her own. Then her father pulled Claire firmly away and lifted her up onto his hip. His free hand guided Rose through the doorway.

Eugénie did not stop him though she heard Claire sobbing. And when the sound of her father's voice, of Claire's sobs, and of Rose's silence had been carried out of the apartment and down and out of reach inside the elevator, she found herself alone in the living room. Not a sound. A car passed in the street below. The silence returned. She became conscious of the clock ticking and did not want to hear it. She covered her ears with her hands. A faint humming started inside her head. She pressed her fingers into her ears. The swollen emptiness hummed louder.

A button was missing from her skirt. She unplugged her ears. The ticking clock, the sound of a passing car flooded in. Madame Lemieux called "*Bonjour*" to someone on the landing. Eugénie stood up and opened the doors to the balcony. There lay the button. It had been torn off earlier, as she lifted her leg over the balcony wall. "You must endure." Those were the words God had spoken to her, and she had lowered her leg, had not let herself drop through the sky. But He, God, had not explained how she was to endure.

From her mending basket she chose a needle, cut a length of thread and forced herself to hold the button in place. The thread disappeared behind the fabric then reappeared. She repeated the movement several times, then pricked her finger with the needle and produced a drop of blood. Tears blurred her vision.

Her father found her shaking, sobbing uncontrollably. "I have left the girls with Madame Vagnard."

"What did you tell them?"

"That Madame Vagnard desired their assistance in preparing a special dessert. When I left, they were removing the stones from cherries."

Eugénie closed her eyes and rested her head against his chest. Her father led her down the hall to her room. Claire and Rose would have no father. Instead they would contain, inside their chests, empty spaces the size of fists. They will reach into those cavities again and again, she told herself. And I? What am I to do?

Her father lifted her feet onto the bed. He held a cup to her lips. "Drink," he said.

When she heard, far off, the large doors in the front hall open and Aunt Sonya call out, "Is no one here?" she opened her eyes. There was the sound of whispering. Footsteps were followed by more words she could not make out. Then the room became dark and soft. Again she slept undisturbed.

At some time Cousin Misha must have come home and then Vera. When she got up they were both in the living room waiting for her, a game of chess taking shape between them. She offered them a smile. She felt the smile violated something inside her, and she went back to bed. Her mother, of course, was away. She was always away. This time to the Alps. Rose? Claire? She pulled off her covers. Madame Lemieux's dessert was surely prepared by now? As she lifted her feet, a wave of exhaustion pressed her into the mattress. Whatever her father had given her to drink was strong. She slept on for an indefinite expanse of time. Then she heard a small voice—"Maman"—and she opened her eyes. Rose and Claire were standing next to her. "Come," she said. They climbed onto the bed. The warmth of their bodies seeped into her own.

WHENEVER SOMEONE PLAYED the cello, Eugénie Balashovskaya thought of Volodya. First, he stood in front of her, holding her hands in his, laughing. Next he sat across from her at the table in their dark Boston dining room, rolling his napkin ring back and forth until the motions of his mind became even. His moustache twitched, ever so slightly. He stood up and went to the living room to play. For him there was no abruptness in his departure, his thoughts having led him off into the room minutes before. Eugénie, observing him, believed she had learned to recognize what his actions meant.

But whatever Volodya did back then, it was coated now with an oily film. These scenes are my inventions, thought Eugénie. She picked up her knitting from where it lay beside her on the sofa. His death has lost the clarity of those orderly words on the telegram. Maybe, she thought, he never existed. She knitted two straight, tight rows. His last breath. He died on another continent, without warning me. Eugénie set down her knitting and checked her radio guide. Yes, it was the Berlin Philharmonic. A bright and sharp note could produce stillness.

THE LARGE DOORS in the hall banged shut. "Hello? Mémère?" Anna appeared, holding out a bouquet.

"These are for you."

"How generous of you, and unnecessary," exclaimed Eugénie. Anna crouched beside the sofa. "Of course it's necessary."

"Little Anna, what do you think? Anemones are my favourite flower. You shouldn't have spent your money. But since you have, I will put these in the dining room and enjoy them."

The telephone rang, urgent, flinging itself in front of Eugénie's slow steps, forcing its way under the tappings of her cane.

"Ah, it is you, *mon petit*. Yes, she is in. She came just now. She brought me a bouquet of anemones." Eugénie turned to Anna.

"Nicholas is on the telephone. He would like to speak with you."

"Thank you, Mémère." Anna took the receiver. "Hello," she said, and sat down. "Yes. Yes, I am free a week Friday. Very well then, until a week Friday, at eight o'clock." She set down the receiver and went into the dining room, where Eugénie stood, arranging her anemones in a glass vase.

"He's asked me to dinner. A week Friday. I am to go to his house and we will leave from there."

"The station nearest Nicholas's house is Tolbiac. I will show you on the map. The neighbourhood isn't wonderful but . . ."

An hour ago, I stood in front of his door, thought Anna.

"The walk from the station will take you ten minutes at most. Come, I will show you on the map."

Anna followed Eugénie into the sitting room and to her desk, forcing her feet to take small, slow steps.

"Sit beside me, *ma petite* Anna, " invited Eugénie.

Nicholas also thinks I am little, a mere child, thought Anna. She brought a chair and sat, but Eugénie stood up.

"May I help?" asked Anna.

"No, *ma petite*. I am going to close the balcony door. Then we will be in peace."

The air became still. The rumble of the city fell away. With her finger, Eugénie traced on the map the route to Nicholas's house.

Twenty-Two

IN THE GARDEN AT ARCELON, the scent of ripe plums and warm earth filled the air. A few indolent clouds hung above the fields. Rose had climbed the ladder and was picking the fruit. Ivan watched her feet, side by side on the narrow rung, and her naked arm reaching among the leaves. He lay down in the grass beneath the tree. "Where are the others?"

"Mary drove them into town."

"All of them?"

"Yes."

"Ah." His head rested in his clasped hands. He shut his eyes and felt the sun's hot breath upon him, the warmth of the earth beneath him. A blade of grass scratched his wrist. He opened his eyes into brilliance. Her arm, naked among the leaves, moved above him. She descended the ladder and sat beside him in the grass. The house behind them, the road to town, the others driving along it, the wall, the gate at the bottom of the garden—all these things were swept aside by the tenderness of her arm. Surrounding her face hung her dark hair, and surrounding her hair stretched the hot blue sky, unquestioning. Ivan sat up and kissed her.

Twenty-Three

THE TABLECLOTHS WERE WHITE and of a daunting beauty. Anna resolved to ignore the arrogant, unsmiling waiters. A pinkness hovered in the light, as if the walls had released particles of their colour.

"Do you really want me to eat a rooster's crest?" she asked.

"I want you to eat anything that will give you pleasure. And I assure you that to eat a rooster's crest is permissible," answered Nicholas.

"How does it taste?"

"The taste is hard to describe. The texture is soft."

"Do *you* like to eat the crest?"

"Very much. But tonight I will have snails."

"Then I will take the rooster's crest."

Anna felt inside the pocket of her dress. The address book lay nestled between folds of cloth.

The waiter appeared. He did not ask Nicholas what he was doing, eating dinner with a young woman dressed in awkward clothing, who had never been held naked in the arms of a naked man. Instead, he described the wines.

Anna stared at Nicholas's small hands and imagined them unbuttoning his shirt, squeezing a tube of toothpaste, turning the page of a book. Then the waiter was gone and Nicholas remained.

"Are you enjoying Paris?" he asked.

"A great deal."

He wanted to know what she was enjoying. The museums? The gardens? The traffic? The libraries? The cinemas? "Have you made friends?" he asked. He paused, his eyes laughing. "Or possibly Frenchmen are not to your liking?"

"I don't know if I like them." She felt, again, the hard address book in her pocket. "I don't know if they like me," she corrected herself. She looked up from the whiteness of the tablecloth, expected to find his mouth amused, but encountered tenderness.

"I've often wondered," Nicholas said, "why Mémère never married again." He had felt Anna struggling, tugging like a fish on his line. He hoped that by mentioning Mémère, he would lift her off his hook and drop her back into her element.

"Do you have a theory about Mémère?" she asked.

"When my grandfather fell dead from a heart attack, Mémère was only thirty years old or so. Perhaps she took a lover." He hesitated. "Why are you smiling?"

"I don't know."

"Does thirty seem old to you?"

"Yes."

"Then I am an old man."

"Yes," she said, "you are." And she grinned at him.

THE ROOSTER'S CREST CAME and she ate it with curiosity. It was delicious, she told him. She did not say that her taste buds were numb with fear, the tips of her fingers chilled.

"Thirty and onwards is much nicer than twenty," said Nicholas. "Less confusing. Life only gets better. You don't believe me, do you? You're still smiling." He proceeded to eat a snail.

The shore seemed far away to Anna. She dived beneath a

wave, surfaced, caught sight of land, still far-removed. She wouldn't reach it. His hand would remain on his side of the white tablecloth. It wouldn't touch hers even though she'd left hers available beside her plate.

She took her hand back, buried it in her skirt where he couldn't see it. When he played the piano it was not for her. The next time his notes travelled down the corridor to her room, she would force herself to stand away from the door and stuff her thumbs in her ears.

"What a smile. Do I amuse you? You're making me nervous," he said.

"This room is beautiful." It was true. It was the only truth she could offer him. The light was peaceful, the room spacious. In its centre grew a tree whose uppermost leaves brushed the ceiling. The perfect waiters, who knew how to hide anything, were passing plates through conversations. A meticulous plan existed behind it all. An elegant restaurant, Anna decided, is a wondrous thing.

"In the summer, if the weather is fine, they open the doors wide," Nicholas said. He showed her with his arms. "They set tables outdoors on the terrace overlooking the park. Then you feel you are inside the park. It is a shame it is still too cold."

But Nicholas did not say, "Will you come here with me, in the summer?" And it did not occur to her that he was also waiting, that the evening lay uncharted ahead of him.

Anna pulled the little book from her pocket and offered it to him, across the table.

"It was my mother's, when she lived here. I stole it."

He examined the outside.

"Open it. The last pages are the most interesting," she told him, and he did as he was told. " 'It was the fault of the rain.' " She quoted the familiar words. "And do you see the llama?"

"I see it."

"What was my mother guilty of?" she asked.

"How should I know?" He handed back the little red book, frowning.

"Your sister says my mother had an affair with Sherbatsky."

"My sister is not always a reliable source of information."

"But my mother could have."

"Yes. She could have, but I doubt she did. What I remember is your mother's smile. It softened the ragged edges of my childhood. She lifted the fog so that I could see farther. I remember the purity of her white hair. I have no reason to suspect your mother of betraying mine. And if she did make love to him, did she necessarily betray my mother?"

"I stole this book from my mother. It was hidden in a drawer among some old postcards and catalogues from art exhibits."

He picked up his dessert fork and spun it between the palms of his hands.

"And I stole the portrait your mother painted of mine." He picked up his knife and buttered a piece of bread. "My sister demanded that Mémère get rid of it, so I took it. Now Barbara claims I 'stole' it. Would you like to see the painting?"

"Yes. Very much."

"Then, some evening I'll invite you to my house to see it."

"Will you?"

"Yes. I am curious to know what you'll think. You will be able to tell me how it compares with the rest of your mother's work."

He is kind to me because I am Mary's daughter, thought Anna. He thinks of me as a younger cousin.

"I don't know much about paintings. My mother hides hers."

"*Ah bon?*"

"They're on the third floor. She won't hang them up. But I have one in my room."

"Why doesn't she display them?"

"She won't say." Anna took a piece of bread and tore it in two. "Is there a story Mémère tells that you like best?" she asked.

Nicholas filled Anna's glass with wine. It's Mémère who

interests her, he decided. She's accepted to have dinner with me because of my family history.

"Has Mémère told you why she was fired by the boarding school in Boston where she taught French?"

"No. Never."

"*Bon.* Then I will tell you. She lasted one year, or perhaps less. She had no idea how to discipline anyone. Her students chattered, drew pictures on their desks, sent each other notes. One day, while she covered the blackboard with declensions, the room fell silent. She turned around: every chair was empty. Her students had climbed out the windows, into the garden. Imagine—the rows of abandoned desks!

"Poor Mémère."

"Yes. Poor Mémère." Nicholas took a sip of wine. "You have a lovely mouth. You make me think of a woman by Renoir."

Fear made Anna's heart beat faster. "Thank you. But I don't like Renoir's women. They are all fat and white."

"*Ah vraiment?* I find them beautiful. And there is something of them in you."

Anna felt his smile lift her hair. His lips brushing across her neck.

"Tell me something else about Mémère. After Boston, what sort of work did she do in Paris?"

"She found work as a translator, for a Scottish whisky company. She began speaking French with a Scottish accent. You are smiling. You don't believe what I'm saying about her accent?"

"No. I don't."

"But I am telling you the truth. Listen to her, carefully. She pronounces every word with a different accent. She liked the men at the Scottish whisky company. So she added one more accent to her linguistic soup. Don't you believe me?" Nicholas smoothed his moustache and waited for her answer. I have not succeeded in calming her, he reflected. The idea of being seduced by an old man over thirty horrifies her.

"Perhaps, I believe you, a little," Anna conceded. She looked down and saw the empty plates. We have eaten all our food, she thought. We have only a small amount of time left.

Nicholas studied Anna's face. "Decidedly, you remind me of one of Renoir's women."

"Thank you. I accept your compliment."

Do you trim your moustache every day? she wanted to ask. The hairs were cut off evenly, each the same length. You have no intention of inviting me to your house to show me the painting, do you?

"My family," said Nicholas and started to fold his napkin into a boat, but stopped himself. He drank the last of his wine, instead. "In my family, everyone is crazy."

He's making a boat, thought Anna.

"Do your parents love each other?" he asked.

She raised her eyes from his hands to his face. You wanted to escape from your family, in a boat made from a napkin, she wanted to say.

"Yes. They love each other," she told him.

"What extraordinary good fortune to have parents who love one another," he said.

The waiters were moving through the soft light in their ironed and starched uniforms. The tablecloths, like the waiters' uniforms, had been pressed free of wrinkles and had had their stains removed. The gentle light that was not pink but gave an impression of pinkness enveloped every conversation.

Life is cruel, thought Anna. I can do nothing to help him, and he can't help me. It's because of this table between us.

"You will have dessert, won't you?" Nicholas asked.

"Will you?"

"At my age I shouldn't."

"You aren't fat."

"No, I'm not fat." He smiled. "But I could easily become so. Once you are thirty years old, you'll see."

"I would like a chocolate mousse, please."

The mousse arrived and Nicholas watched Anna eat it. She felt her lips belonged to someone else. Sweet chocolate coated her tongue. A tingle spread down her neck and along her arms.

Then it was her turn to watch. Nicholas took a packet of cigars from his breast pocket. "Would you like one?"

"Please."

He handed her a cigar. It was slender, not so thick as she had expected. As he lighted it, a peculiar taste, similar to the smell of damp pavement on a hot day, filled her mouth. They sat, facing each other, smoking.

Twenty-Four

WHILE NICHOLAS DROVE, ANNA SAT BESIDE HIM, her knee separated from his by a small amount of air. She watched his hand move the gearshift and saw how close his fingers came to touching her stocking. She wondered if her stockings made her legs attractive to him, more adult. Whenever she pulled on stockings she felt as though she were burying her legs alive; when she peeled them off at night, her legs breathed again. There was not enough traffic to prevent their evening from coming to an end. Long, lighted windows in buildings sailed past. Soon Nicholas would park his car. He would return her, untouched, to Mémère's apartment. The Pont de Bir-Hakeim came into view. Above the bridge a Métro train glided through the air. Below, cars crossed the river, their headlights unblinking.

NICHOLAS STEPPED OUT of the car and opened Anna's door. She emerged and held out her hand. He laughed, ignoring her hand, and kissed her on both cheeks.

"*Ma petite Anglaise*. Thank you for a most agreeable evening."

"I should thank you."

"I'll wait until you are safely inside."

She didn't move. You can't make me move, she thought. Say it—I don't love you, Anna. You're pretty, but you're young and unsophisticated.

"I was robbed once, exactly here," he explained.

"By whom?"

"A boy with a knife."

"You weren't hurt?"

"No. I wasn't hurt. I lost some money, and that's not important."

"I am glad you weren't hurt. Good night." She pressed in the code on the small metal buttons to the right of the doors. She stood in the courtyard, listening until he started the engine of his car.

Twenty-Five

THROUGH HIS GRANDMOTHER'S dining room windows, Nicholas stared at the ugly new apartment blocks on the opposite bank of the Seine. They looked as if they had been dropped from the air, without thought for love or beauty. It was not the first time he'd seen them. They had existed for ten years. This afternoon he was staring at these ugly edifices out of exhaustion. He could have looked in the other direction, chosen beauty, the Eiffel Tower, the gold dome of the Invalides. But today it was ugliness that intrigued him, and he counted their windows. Some sixty to one hundred families were condemned to inhabit such sterility. And they were among the fortunate.

The clock in the hall struck four. He set two coffee cups on the table, two tiny gold spoons, the heavy sugar bowl. A week had elapsed since he'd had dinner with Anna. He'd thought about her often and with curiosity in the past week. Today, however, his thoughts were preoccupied with the frustrations of his career. He put dessert plates and forks on the table.

Paris is a labyrinth containing a secret room, he mused. Within this room, a table has been set. Musicians, philosophers, painters, physicists, writers, and possibly a handful of doctors are engaged in conversation. They are the best. *Les forts*. They are juggling ideas, colourful and brilliant as gems. The tinkling of crystal is heard. It is a room suffused with light. I want to find the door to that room, Nicholas told himself. If I could locate the door, would the handle turn?

They all have passed a rigorous test to enter. I want to be put to the test. I would like to get close enough to the door, at least to overhear their conversation. Once, last year, I thought the door was in front of me, the handle turned, I stepped in, but the room was all wrong. Grandet, my esteemed colleague, was seated alone, a white rat eating cake crumbs from his hand.

FROM THE HALL came the squeak of metal wheels. Nicholas got up. He relieved Mémère of her Cadillac and guided it through the narrow door.

"What a splendid tart! You shouldn't have gone to the trouble," he told her. Then he yawned. "Forgive me." He stretched and yawned again. "I have been up late."

"Are you in love?"

"Do you wish I were? I have stayed up reading." He imagined Anna crossing the Place de la Sorbonne, arm in arm with a young man, a student her age. Am I in love? Perhaps I am. And Barbara is filling Anna's head with suspicions. "It was the fault of the rain." What was? A head of a llama? Sherbatsky sketched at the zoo, and apparently so did Mary. What does that prove? Barbara claims she once saw him touch Mary's neck. Did he? Barbara was jealous of Mary. She's jealous of me. What else has she told Anna? The same lies she told Janine? That I am a seducer, a collector of women?

"I also keep myself up too late, reading," said Eugénie, watching him cut the tart. "Why don't you shave off your moustache?"

"Because I like my moustache."

"It makes you look like every other man with a moustache."

"I like my moustache, and I will not shave it off." He passed her a slice of her tart, adding, "Your husband had a moustache."

"That is true. And I did not like his either," she answered, standing up.

"Where are you going?"

"To get the cream."

"We don't need cream. Neither your heart nor my waist requires cream." But she had already passed through the doors.

Nicholas thought of the small room, where radiant ideas glanced off one another. I must publish, he told himself.

Mémère put the cream on the table.

Twenty-Six

While Nicholas drank his coffee, Barbara very nearly drove into a white van. She was determined to arrive at Eugénie's before Nicholas left. Mémère had said she expected him for coffee at four o'clock.

All the same, I must calm down before I drive any farther, she told herself. And by good fortune, she found a parking spot. Two wheels raised on the sidewalk, she sat in her tilted car, rewinding her feelings. Was she prepared to expose them to Nicholas? An old conversation started up in her head.

"Nicholas, Maman killed herself."

"She fell into the river. She was balancing on the wall of the Pont d'Austerlitz, the wind tugged at her hat and she reached up. That's all we know."

"I pity your patients."

"I might come to a different conclusion about a patient. But we are discussing Maman."

"I know whom we are discussing. I started this discussion."

"How do you hope to end it?"

"By having you admit that Maman killed herself."

"She drowned in the Seine. She lost her balance. You are free to make your own interpretation."

"She fell into a river rather than buy a new straw hat with a ribbon around it? How can you deceive yourself, Nicholas? Isn't it your job to dig out the truth?"

"Barbara. I must get going."

WILL I HAVE THAT SAME CONVERSATION today? There's nothing more I can do to convince Nicholas. He prefers to remain blind. I'm ready to let him have his way—two endings, two versions of the "truth," if that will please him. I've taken my little revenge on innocent Anna. I've told her what I saw. What is she thinking? I'm not going to worry about that. It will be best for her if she does find out the truth. I'm tired of fighting with Nicholas. Liuba's right that hating him is futile.

Barbara drove off the sidewalk and into the brilliant sunlight of the late afternoon.

Twenty-Seven

As Nicholas emerged from Eugénie's building, Barbara pulled up in her car. He watched her extricate herself from the driver's seat.

"Nicholas."

"*Bonjour.*"

They kissed. He felt in his pocket for his car keys.

You smell familiar, thought Barbara, but you don't look the way I expected you to. You look older.

She stood in front of him, her hands at her sides. A few feet away climbed two great pillars of metal, painted silver. They supported the bridge on which the trains of the Métro crossed high above the streets and the river.

"*Quelle coïncidence! Comment vas-tu?*" Nicholas asked.

"I want to speak to you."

"Can I call you? I have a patient waiting and I am late."

"Do we have to be enemies?"

"No. I don't want to be your enemy." A deafening rumble. The train rolled along its rails above their heads.

"You can think what you like about Maman and how she died. You have a right to," Barbara shouted into the noise.

"Barbara, I want to speak with you," he shouted back, "but right now I must go."

In the wake of the train the street became quiet.

Barbara did not see her brother's smile. She looked at his tidy feet in their polished shoes. He did not have time to speak with her; he had said so. She studied his clothes—the white linen vest, the brown corduroy trousers, casual yet elegant, the result of calculation. He had time to dress but not to speak with her. Her gaze glided from his tense shoulders up to his face, which now wore a puzzled expression.

"May I call you this evening?" he asked.

He doesn't have time to speak to me, yet he has the time to dress with great care. The idea beat inside her skull. She didn't care if she was ignoring circumstance, comparing a morning and an afternoon event. In the morning he'd cared to dress well; this afternoon he didn't care to speak with her. And why was he late? Why did he have no time?

"You can't stop to listen because you're late. Mémère kept you. It's her fault, someone else's fault. The fault is never yours. Your errors melt in the heat of your importance and you don't see them any more. You mould them into something else."

"Barbara, did you want to talk about Maman?"

"Yes!"

"I can't talk now, but I will call you tonight. May I? Will you be in?"

"I want to talk to you about her now."

"I will phone you." Nicholas started to walk away. Something hard hit him on the back between his shoulder blades. He stopped, stunned. Barbara pounded him again, this time on the side of his neck. She was using as her weapon a jar of chestnut purée pulled from the depths of her purse. The purée had been intended as a present for Mémère.

"Stop it!" he shouted. She hit him once more. He grabbed her hair, pulling her away from him. She screamed. They faced each other. On the opposite sidewalk, a man, holding a leash with a squat, frizzy white dog attached to the end of it, stared at them.

"How could you?" she shouted.

"You hit me first."

Another train rolled over the bridge, burying them beneath its rumbling and rattling.

"You never listen to me!"

"I have listened to you for hour upon hour!"

"And heard nothing!"

Nicholas didn't answer. He walked to his car, unlocked it and got in.

He started to drive off. Barbara's jar of chestnut purée crashed against his rear window, shattered the glass, bounced off the trunk, then rolled along the pavement. Nicholas continued to drive.

Barbara watched his car disappear around the corner. She walked back and stood in front of the tall glass doors with their black metal curls. The code to open the doors should have been located somewhere in her mind. She couldn't find it. She stood and waited. But no one opened the doors from the inside. She could have rung the concierge's bell, but she realized she had no reason to visit Mémère. She had nothing offer, no chestnut purée.

Where should she go?

She considered driving to Liuba's, but remembered that Liuba would be at the hospital, working. She got into her car, and cried.

Twenty-Eight

EUGÉNIE WASHED HER CUP AND PLATE, then Nicholas's. Next, she went into her bedroom. She found the box, out of reach on top of her armoire. First she pushed the stool from her dressing table across the room, then climbed up. She reached with the handle of her hairbrush. Triumph. The dislodged box fell to the floor with a thud. All that remained was to retrieve it. She began her descent, gripping the door of the armoire. Her feet, then after more painful effort her knees, touched the floor.

She opened the box and lifted the tissue paper. Rose's wedding dress had withstood time. With the tip of her finger, Eugénie traced the scalloped collar, caressed the small roundness of the buttons.

"Rose," she said.

The dress looked nothing like her daughter. Rose had been neither pale nor delicate. Her bones were heavy, her face broad, her hair wiry. Rose's eyes were the colour of a fine rain, but unsettled as the ocean. Eugénie hid the dress under the tissue paper. To continue to look at it was to run the risk of believing that Rose had been pale, delicate as lace.

God manifested Himself in Rose. Now her body is gone, but that should not matter, Eugénie told herself. What was

Godlike in Rose continues to exist. I hear it in the music of Mozart and of Schubert. I see it in the beauty of my plants.

But I want to hold her hand. I want to speak with her. I am not strong enough to love only God. Must I look harder for Him? Must I love even Josette, my concierge? I can find nothing Godlike in Josette.

Eugénie sat down on the stool, the box on her knees. Why François Kelman? she asked. Why didn't Rose marry some other man? She knew she should not ask. The past is no longer. Truth is to be found in the present.

In her imagination, she heard Nicholas say, "My mother's father died when she was a child. Therefore, she wanted a wounded man."

"Who in a capitalist society can act morally?" complained Léon.

"Are you excusing François?" asked Claire.

"Of course I am not. I'm merely pointing out that his cowardly treatment of Rose was symptomatic of capitalist society."

"Léon, do you believe what you are saying?" asked Claire.

"So long as we have capitalism we will have plenty of Françoises."

"Of course, we are all wounded," said Nicholas. "But my mother chose someone more wounded than the majority of men. If one can say she chose."

They were all chattering at her. They would not stop. There remained the enormous task of returning the box to the top of the armoire. Eugénie shoved the box under her bed. They went on, and on, arguing.

"My mother—" Nicholas began. But Eugénie interrupted him.

"Rose married a wounded man because she had lost her father, but why did her father die?" she asked.

"I don't know," said Nicholas.

Still in her imagination, Eugénie noticed Léon squeezing Claire's hand. Léon was a good man, always marching for peace or collecting signatures to free someone. Once he'd explained to her about the English taking away land from innocent Scottish peasants, how they'd passed a law called the Enclosures Act. His knowledge was broad, a vast boulevard leading towards a fixed point on the horizon—the redistribution of wealth.

Eugénie pushed the upholstered stool across the room. She arrived at her dressing table. Does Anna know about the Scottish peasants? If not, I will tell her.

Tiredness and sorrow took hold of her and shook her empty. She sat on her stool and listened to the clock on her mantelpiece.

IN THE SITTING ROOM she pulled a shining black record from its paper sleeve. She turned the small red dial on the record player, and the plastic arm, holding the needle, lifted itself up. By the time she'd arrived at the sofa, the music had started. She listened, and then she must have closed her eyes, for when she opened them, the room was dark and the record was turning round and round, no sound coming out.

She pulled herself up and crossed the room. She returned the needle to the record's rim, to the beginning. She sat down, once more. First came the violin, then the cello joined in, and notes fell one by one from the piano. They tumbled, gathered themselves, caught hold and climbed.

Twenty-Nine

Barbara had undressed, taken a play from her shelf and climbed into bed when the telephone rang.

"What have I done?" asked Nicholas.

"Don't you know, doctor?"

"Please. Barbara. Stop waving my profession in my face as though it were a warrant for my arrest. If I knew what crime I'd committed, I wouldn't ask. Tell me what I'm guilty of. Explain it to me."

Should she explain? It was late. She'd spent her evening crying.

"You wouldn't listen," she said. "That's your crime. I came to tell you our argument was over, that we wouldn't mention Maman's death again. You rushed off and I hit you. I behaved horribly. I have a talent for that. I behaved like a child. And I hated myself for it. But there was a reason I hit you."

"I understood that you came to tell me you wanted to make peace. I was astounded. But I was also late for an appointment. Yes, you behaved like a child. That doesn't make you horrible."

Barbara wrapped the telephone cord around her finger. In her mind, Nicholas stood in the stairwell off the kitchen, about to climb the narrow wooden stairs past the garbage chute, up to the *chambre de bonne* that was his new domain. The *chambre de bonne* was his because he'd asked for it, though she was older than him by two years.

His foot was raised ready to climb away from her, to give himself to his girlfriend or to his books, to whatever waited up there, to his cigarettes and politics and friends, all up there, waiting for him. She had to remain below, with Mémère, in the empty rooms with their unbearably beautiful view.

"You didn't listen," she repeated.

A blank silence travelled through the wires. An infinite possibility and an emptiness.

"You're right. I didn't stop to talk. I can only say that I'm sorry. I wasn't able to."

"Are you apologizing?"

"Yes."

"I accept your apology. Thank you."

"You're welcome."

He was fourteen, at the front door, a suitcase hanging from his hand. He'd decided to take the train to visit their father, although she'd pleaded with him not to. Didn't he care that Maman was dead, that she'd be alive if it weren't for their father? She stared at the suitcase, willing it to open, to spill his socks and underwear onto the floor.

"It is late. I'm glad we've spoken. Good night, Barbara," said Nicholas.

She put down the receiver, then picked it up and listened to the empty wires humming.

She was eighteen. From the balcony she looked down on his dark head. His school books were bulging from the bag slung over his shoulder. He was sixteen. The slate-coloured rooftops of the city hid more terrors than delights. That is what she believed. She watched him cross the road and start over the Pont de Bir-Hakeim. Midway, where the bridge widened, a girl was waiting for him. Nicholas took the girl in his arms and kissed her.

How long did I wait for him to finish kissing that girl? Barbara wondered. She put down the receiver and the humming ceased.

In the kitchen, she pulled a tin of paint from under the sink. With a screwdriver, she pried off the lid. She stirred the pigment from the bottom, using a piece of flat wood. When the paint was even in colour, a cream of cauliflower soup, she carried it into the living room where she threw a sheet over the sofa. She set up her ladder and climbed.

Thirty

Mary stepped away from the canvas. "It's not right yet. I'm sorry. And I can't do any more today. If I keep at it, I'll ruin it. Will you come another day, and sit one more time?"

"Of course I'll come," said Rose.

"I'll put on the kettle. Can you stay a bit?"

"A few minutes. I promised Barbara I would take her shopping for a new pair of shoes. She says I'm never around any more."

"That's not true, is it?"

"My thoughts are often elsewhere."

Mary thrust her brushes into the turpentine. She filled the kettle.

"Is it Ivan?"

"Yes. He doesn't plan to marry me... That wouldn't matter if I were sure he was going to stay in Paris. But he says that Paris will never be home."

"He won't leave you."

"You don't think so?"

"He told me that he wants to go to New York some day, and I asked him if he would take you with him, and Nicholas and

Barbara." Mary worked the brushes in the turpentine, then pulled them out and dried them on her rag.

"What did he answer?"

"Yes. If you were willing."

Rose's lips curved in a tired smile. Her eyes remained anxious. "And live off what, in New York? He says, yes he'd take us, because he knows it's impossible. He doesn't want to stay in one place, or with one woman." Rose turned off the heat under Mary's kettle and poured the water into the teapot. She wandered to the windows. There wasn't a cloud in the sky. She felt Mary looking at her and she turned.

"I'll have to go back to Canada soon," said Mary. She was studying her friend. The shape of her mouth, the width between her cheekbones, the form of her nose. "I'll never capture you."

"I think you will. How soon are you leaving? You didn't tell me."

"Not for another four months. That's why I haven't said anything. I don't like to think about it."

"May I look at the painting?" asked Rose.

Thirty-One

"CLAIRE?"

Claire opened her eyes. "Was I sleeping?"

"We have both been taking a nap," explained Eugénie.

"I suppose I was tired. *Ça fait du bien.*" Claire looked across the room. Above the balcony hung the bandaged sky. Indoors the clocks ticked. The plants spilled over the marble mantel of the fireplace. She wriggled her stiff shoulders and stood up.

"Your bills are paid," she told her mother. "I'll drop them in a letterbox on my way home."

"Thank you, Claire."

Eugénie made no effort to stand. "I am growing lazy. I have never been a hard worker. Sonya used to shake her head when she read my homework. I was not a good student." She shifted position in her chair.

"Are you uncomfortable, Maman?"

"A little. Last year when I worked as a volunteer at the library, I got more exercise. I glued in the loose pages; but there were so few borrowers, I would fall asleep. They were afraid that one day I might not wake up." Eugénie's laugh exploded into the room.

Claire stood with her mother's bills in her hand. I hope you die suddenly, thought Claire, that you don't spend years as an invalid.

"With so few borrowers," said Eugénie, "I found the library dull. But I could not leave. A small Christian library—they might have had difficulty replacing me. The churches are not needed now. People have other ways of judging each other. They meet elsewhere."

"Do we meet?" asked Claire, pulling herself into the present. "Léon and I attend countless gatherings, my Retired Engineers, the Green Party, Léon's geologists. Our calendar is scribbled with encounters. We all talk at once and complain. We produce a pamphlet. We hope to be heard, that we will cause a petrified thought to be unearthed inside someone's head. But do we meet?"

"Mr. Strang said we meet in God, that there is no external God. If God is love, He is the human experience of it." Eugénie felt an intense itching at the back of her neck. She tried to reach the spot but could not.

"Maman, do you ever wish you hadn't let Nicholas take the portrait of Rose?" asked Claire. "The one by Mary Bertram that hung in the dining room."

"Barbara detested it. She asked me to take it down."

"I miss it." Claire picked up the glass egg from her mother's desk. When you die, I'll be alone, she thought. No father. No sister, no mother, no children of my own. Only Léon.

"Shall I ask Nicholas to let you have it for a while?"

"*Non, Maman. Ça ne vaut pas la peine.*"

"Barbara has offered to pay for his car window, but he's refused," remarked Eugénie.

Claire set down the egg. She felt suddenly drained of energy.

"I've failed Rose. That's what I think sometimes, Maman. When you told me about the chestnut purée, I felt frightened. At the same time I wanted to laugh. What have I done to help them? Could I have changed their lives?"

"You did what you could, *ma chérie*. You couldn't become

Rose. Don't think such thoughts." Eugénie pulled herself out of the green settee. She walked to the table and peered around a teetering pile of books nestled between the quietly breathing plants.

"Are you looking for something, Maman?"

"My watering can."

"Your plants have already been watered. I felt the soil. Perhaps Josette watered them when she was cleaning?"

Eugénie continued her search. "Perhaps Josette has broken my watering can." She spotted the plastic vessel. It was perched on top of the piano, yellow as a canary, surrounded by sheet music. "The piano is no place for a watering can." She lifted down her treasure. "And my blue milk pitcher... Josette claims she didn't break it. But I can find no sign of it." The lead weights tugged at her ankles, and she succumbed, accepting the green settee. "And who is weeding my garden at Arcelon? No one. Will you take me there soon?"

"*Oui, Maman.*"

Time crawls, thought Eugénie, inside this apartment.

Thirty-Two

Barbara slammed the door, pulled off her coat and threw it on the bed. She did not greet Sarah, Delphine, or George, nor did she lift the dolls from their cushions on the floor so that they might look out the window into the street below.

"Damn that man," she said, dialing Liuba's telephone number. Her finger dragged the little wheel, released it, tugged it again. It all took so long. She held her breath. A bell rang twice in quick succession across the city.

"*Allô?*"

"Liuba? It's me. He was waiting outside my door."

"Your concierge?"

"Yes. Today he couldn't find anything on the landing to repair, so he slumped against the wall and closed his eyes, as if he were resting. He waited for me to come home, then he watched me unlock my door. *Il ne fait que m'en merder! Quel con.*"

"When was this?"

"Just now."

"Is he still out there?"

"I don't know."

"Will you go and look while I'm on the line?"

LIUBA LISTENED TO BARBARA'S FOOTSTEPS grow faint. She heard, beneath the silence, an alarmed fluttering of wings. But this time the bird wasn't caught in Barbara's chest; it was the sound of her own fear.

"He's gone," declared Barbara.

"Good."

"I detest him."

"Is he likely to come back?"

"No. I don't think so. Not today."

"Is Henri in town?"

"He's in London again. What does Henri have to do with it?"

"I want you to be safe."

"Liuba..."

"Could you move into Henri's place while he's away?"

"I'll be fine."

"You've convinced me I should worry."

"Henri is Henri. This is my apartment. I live here."

"I want to know you're safe."

"I am not going to be chased out by some lazy, not very bright weirdo who falls asleep on the landing."

"He was watching you. He waited for you."

"I've repainted half the living room. That's what I was really calling to tell you. I've climbed the ladder. I've done it."

"You did? That's wonderful."

"And I had a horrible fight with my brother. But he has apologized to me."

"What happened?"

"I'll tell you when I see you."

"I'd be happier if you'd come and stay with me. Then I'd know you were safe."

"I shouldn't have called. You're starting to think I'm one of your invalids."

"We're all invalids."

"That's what my brother says. 'Everyone is crazy.' He's right and he's not right. Liuba, I didn't mean to frighten you. I'm sorry. But I'm not going to run away. On Saturday, are we going to the flea market at Vanves?"

"Yes." She's not going to listen to me any more than my patients do, or than I listen to Maman, Liuba decided. Barbara won't give up either the Samaritaine or her apartment. It's rare that someone saves someone else. When Barbara grabbed my arm on the platform, that was the exception.

"I'm hoping for photos. An ambrotype," said Barbara. "For that sort of thing Vanves is best. There should be lots of old librettos and theatre programs. I'm sure you'll find something for your mother."

"Barbara, will you look and make sure he hasn't come back?"

"No. I don't want to think about him anymore."

"*Bon.* I'll see you on Saturday."

BARBARA SET DOWN THE RECEIVER. She could feel George watching her. The wooden doll sat on her cushion on the floor, the shiny black toes of her painted shoes pointing at the ceiling. Her small eyes expressed disapproval. The smile on her pretty lips would remain half-formed forever. Barbara took her coat from the bed and hung it up. I'm not in love with Henri. It's obvious. The idea landed in her mind, clear and perfect as a drop of rain: I want to stay in this apartment.

Thirty-Three

SHIFTING HER BAG OF BOOKS TO HER HIP, Anna unlocked the door. A sack of groceries swung from her hand. She'd stopped at the market in rue de Seine on her way home from the library. Eggplant and courgettes, yet again. She could think of nothing else to cook.

"Anna?"

There is no point in cooking, she thought. Nicholas doesn't love me.

"Anna?"

She followed Eugénie's voice and found her seated on the green settee.

"Anna, will you sit with me a moment?"

Anna sat down on a worn brown velvet chair. She dropped the sack of groceries and her books at her feet. He doesn't love me. He doesn't love me, she chanted to herself. I will never hear him play again. Never hear him play again. He won't show me the painting. He won't. Ever.

"Anna, tell me about your day."

"I went to the library and on the way home I bought some groceries." She longed to put her head in Mémère's lap and ask,

"Why can't he love me?" To stop herself from doing so, she asked, "Mémère, will you tell me the story of your father's suitcase?"

"Which suitcase, little Anna?"

"The suitcase that was small but weighed so much, and your father longed to set it down but couldn't."

"Ah, the little suitcase," Eugénie began, straightening her spine, setting her hands in readiness upon her knees. "We were travelling by ship from Kiev to France. My mother disliked trains. We crossed the Black Sea and passed through the straits at Constantinople. My father told my mother we could not stop in Greece, because of the little suitcase. She was displeased. The suitcase weighed a great deal. It never left my father's side. Can you imagine, little Anna, what it contained?"

"I've forgotten, Mémère. Tell me." This was Anna's favourite moment in the story; the moment when Mémère's voice and eyes always filled with excitement.

"The suitcase," announced Eugénie, in triumph, "was filled with gold. My father used part of that gold to buy this apartment." Eugénie's laugh shook the leaves of the plants. In the long windows, the wind tossed and teased the curtains. Far below, a boy on a motorcycle raced his engine.

"Little Anna, shouldn't you put away your groceries?"

"Yes, Mémère." Why should I put away my groceries when Nicholas doesn't love me? Why should I? Tell me that.

Thirty-Four

From the front of the Café du Marche patrons could observe the market in the rue de Seine, where citizens of all ages searched for the sweetest carrots, the firmest cauliflower, the lowest prices. At certain times of day, the view was blocked by vans unloading smoked hams and dead chickens, or by trucks delivering cases of soft drinks to the Uni Prix on the corner. But such interruptions were short lived.

Every Tuesday a man named Gerrard claimed one of the front row seats. He had long legs and long fingers. Settled there from noon until four, he waited in the hope that a certain young woman would arrive at the market. On Tuesdays that she failed to appear, a sadness fell from the air into his beer. He would drain his glass and order another. He didn't know the young woman's name, but her occasional absences from the market told him he was fated to spend life alone.

She was a student, and possibly a foreigner—Irish or Scottish, he guessed, from her colouring. Her red-gold hair hung perfectly straight to her waist. On fair days, he enjoyed watching the sun ignite her hair. There was an awkwardness to the way she dressed. She hid her feet inside heavy walking shoes. She wore no lipstick, no eye shadow. On those Tuesdays when she appeared, she purchased her vegetables and walked away with a quick, determined air. He'd come to depend upon her. Between one o'clock and three o'clock there were other women he depended upon, but at three-thirty, he relied upon this girl with the persimmon hair.

Thirty-Five

IN THE SUNLIGHT STREAMING through the windows, Barbara's dark hair shone and her eyes laughed.

"Henri is back."

"So, he has finished his project in London?"

Barbara thrust a small parcel, wrapped loosely in white grocer's paper, into Eugénie hands.

"Yes. These are for you. The first of the season. And I've painted two walls of my living room, Mémère. I've done it, I've climbed my ladder. And Henri's brought me a tea cup with roses in the bottom and on the saucer." Barbara followed Mémère from the sitting room into the round dining room.

"The roses are delicate, an exquisite pink. He says London's sprawling and chaotic but full of surprises."

"What have you brought me? Let me open it," said Eugénie, placing the white parcel on the table in front of her. "My fingers don't want obey me any more. Ah, persimmons. Thank you, *ma petite*. I'll have one with my lunch." Eugénie smiled.

"You must tell me if they aren't ripe. The grocer assured me they were. If they aren't, I'll complain."

"I will eat one, then tell you if your grocer is to be trusted or not." Eugénie felt a sudden pain in her calf, as if a hot nail were being hammered into the bone. Her chest tightened. She lowered herself onto a dining room chair. It is my thinking, she told herself. My Wrong Thinking.

"Are you all right?" asked Barbara.

"*Oui, ma petite.* It is my leg, or rather my thoughts. It will pass." She grimaced. The pain did not altogether ease, but the shock had passed and she was able to breathe more freely.

"Can't I do something? Should I call your doctor?"

"No. It is stopping now. I also have a piece of English china. Claire brought it for me. It is a teapot made of bone china. What do you think they mixed into the clay?"

"Tell me."

"They put a powder of crushed bones. Claire didn't say whose bones."

"Mémère, is it better?"

"*Oui, ma petite.*"

"Let's eat one of the persimmons, now, Mémère. I want to know if the grocer cheated me or not." Barbara lifted one of the weighty orange-red fruits.

"Will Henri take you to London for your honeymoon?"

"I don't know, Mémère." Barbara called this over her shoulder from the hall. In the kitchen, she rinsed the persimmon and dried it. She returned to the dining room and crouched beside her grandmother, the persimmon cradled in her hands.

"When will I meet him?" asked Eugénie.

"I don't want to marry Henri." The words hopped out of her and skipped about the room. Catch me. Catch me! they cried. Barbara blushed. She felt light as a sparrow.

"Have you told him?"

"No, Mémère." Barbara studied the legs of the table.

"When will you tell him?"

"I don't know." Barbara set the persimmon on the table. Her arms felt heavy. The fruit looked perfect.

"If you don't love him, you are doing best not to marry him.

Do you love him, *ma petite?*" said Eugénie. The ache in her calf had diminished to a dull throb.

"I don't think so, Mémère. I feel tired." Barbara sliced open the persimmon and dipped in her spoon. "It *is* ripe," she cried. "The grocer didn't lie to me. Taste it, Mémère. It's ever so sweet. You must eat it all. It's for you."

Thirty-Six

"We are grateful to Dr. Kelman for having agreed to speak to us on such short notice. He will address us on the subject of anxiety in the workplace. Dr. Kelman's most recent paper..."

The introduction over, the audience applauded politely. Nicholas walked with precise, energetic steps across the stage. Could it be? wondered Liuba. Yes, it must be him. There is the famous moustache.

"I will begin by examining a few of the collective defence strategies against anxiety, resorted to by workers exposed to danger," Nicholas began. "In the petrochemical industry, instances abound of workers engaging in potentially fatal amusements. Picture a group of workers on a night shift, holding an illicit banquet. Wine is served. They release steam at 800 degrees Celsius to see how fast they can cook a pork chop. The meat is done in one second flat and consumed amidst laughter. By toying with danger, they have acquired a false sense of security. A week later, these same workers ambush a colleague whom they knock to the ground with the spray from a high-powered fire extinguisher. They have misused the safety equipment so as to invalidate the idea any danger exists."

Liuba listened with interest. Nicholas's discourse ended amidst applause and was followed by lunch.

During lunch, Liuba hoped for a chance to introduce herself but she was kept prisoner at her table by a talkative acquaintance. At two o'clock, she presented a paper on asthma and her colleagues responded with enthusiasm.

As she was buttoning her raincoat at the end of the day, Nicholas approached her.

"Excuse me. Doctor Zaitsev?"

"Yes?"

"I enjoyed your talk."

"Thank you. And I found yours intriguing."

"That's generous of you."

A few minutes of conversation revealed that they had several professional acquaintances in common. They'd reached the doors and they stepped outside.

"May I offer you a drink? If you have the time and you'd accept, I'd be honoured," said Nicholas.

"I have a little bit of time, and I accept with pleasure."

They crossed the road and settled at a small table in a noisy café, recommended only by its proximity.

"I can't stand cigarette smoke," said Liuba.

"*Ah bon?* Shall we find somewhere else?"

"No. The other cafés won't be any better." Liuba smiled at him. The waiter took their order. "Do you know Philipe Grandet? He's still at the Hôtel Dieu, isn't he?" she asked.

"Yes. He's still there."

"He was on the jury when I defended my doctoral thesis," explained Liuba. She twisted her ring around her finger. She tried to guess Nicholas's opinion of Grandet, then added, "I can't say I'm fond of him."

"He's unbearable," said Nicholas with relief. As she lifted her glass he noticed the fine bones of her wrist.

Finished with the topic of their colleagues, they compared their arduous and ugly quests for funding. Nicholas felt her studying his face, her unusual, black eyes bright with amusement. He didn't care if he was the object of her friendly and silent mirth. It wasn't every day a woman examined him with such intensity. The fragility of her pale wrists, the shape and the dark intelligence of her eyes, her wide mouth appealed to him. He wanted to ask her how she'd occupied herself on rainy days, as a child? Did she have any siblings? Did she play the piano? He said her name inside his head—Liuba Zaitsev.

"Is your family Russian?" he asked. "I hope you don't mind my asking? My grandmother was born in Kiev."

He felt an absurd urge to tell this stranger his family's history, to burden her with the story of his childhood. He was experiencing a curious sensation that she knew already what he was about to tell her.

"I was born in Moscow but we moved to Toulouse when I was two," Liuba explained.

"My sister speaks some Russian," said Nicholas. "But I, regrettably, don't."

Although Liuba smiled at him knowingly, she said nothing. To fill the odd silence, Nicholas added, "I won't tell you too much about my sister, or you'll come to the conclusion that everyone in my family is mad."

"How intriguing," exclaimed Liuba. "Please do tell me about your sister, and I will tell you if I think you are all mad."

An hour slipped away as Nicholas offered up his family's dramatic history for Liuba's entertainment. Then she consulted her watch.

"It's so late. I had no idea. I'm afraid I must go," she apologized. "I have someone waiting for me at home."

"Ah?" Nicholas pulled out his wallet. Not only have I bored her, he concluded, but she isn't even single. What a fool I am!

"My mother is waiting for me," admitted Liuba, and she saw him revive. And what do I think of him? She shook the question, as if it were a glass-covered scene, full of pretend snow.

The answers drifted about, twirled down. "He is Barbara's detestable brother" stood like a signpost in the centre of the scene.

"Some other evening, if you are free, and have made no commitment to your mother, would you do me the honour of joining me for dinner?" Nicholas asked.

"Yes," answered Liuba, "with pleasure."

Thirty-Seven

No sooner had Eugénie closed her eyes than she saw his face. His cheeks were rosy. Two hazel eyes examined her own, longer than was polite. In his hand he held a telegram. He should have said it was for her. But he held it out, mutely. He was young. Perhaps newly hired, poorly trained. His shyness appealed to her.

She could allow herself to desire him for these few seconds. Her husband was on the other side of the Atlantic Ocean. How surprising to feel hunger for a boy. She read the telegram. Volodya was dead. She was no longer a married woman but a woman alone.

"Is there any reply?" the boy asked. These were the first words he spoke. His voice, low and scraping at the start, broke without warning, soared high and clear as a flute.

"No," she answered. "There is no reply." To whom could she reply? She read the telegram a second time. It was signed by a friend of Volodya's. But still, she had no reply.

She did not close the door. She did not act.

The boy bent at the waist in a half-bow. Then he straightened up and walked to the stairs and descended them two at a time.

EUGÉNIE OPENED HER EYES and stared at the chocolate-coloured swirls of the marble mantelpiece. Yes, this was the same living room she'd wandered into after that boy left.

Anna must find herself a young man, she thought, and switched on her radio.

Thirty-Eight

IN THE TEA ROOM OF THE MOSQUE, a large and elaborate brass lamp hung by a chain from the centre of the ceiling.

"We must celebrate," Barbara said as she set down her purse on the bench beside her. "I have painted my entire living room."

Arabic music undulated from a cassette player. The notes travelled from the velvet cushions to the brass trays, up and across the ornate ceiling.

The sweetness of the mint tea rushed into Liuba's blood. Since yesterday, a hurrying sensation had inhabited her. The urgency of a secret? Or was it desire? The music of a distant country scoured by hot winds now wrapped itself around her. In her mind Nicholas unknotted his necktie and pulled it off. He undid the top button of his shirt. Yesterday I didn't want to undress him, not yesterday, thought Liuba. She touched her pale hand to her flushed cheek.

"Has something happened?" asked Barbara.

"Yes. Something has happened." Liuba willed the heavy lamp to drop, to smash on the floor. Then they could all scream, and start again with clarity. A woman at the next table lighted a cigarette and, parting her lips, blew an acrid cloud into the room's air. This, thought Liuba, is the start of my punishment. But for what am I being punished? He's her brother, not her lover.

"I have met your brother."

"Where?"

"At a conference. There was a change in the program. He spoke."

"Does he know . . . that you're my friend?"

"No. But he has asked me out to dinner, and I've accepted. I'll tell him then."

Liuba swallowed the rest of her tea. Not since the oral examinations she'd endured as a medical student had she felt so corroded by anxiety. All the little streams of doubt and guilt trickling deep inside her were merging into a single torrent. First she'd deceived Nicholas by inviting him to tell her his life story and not letting on she knew it already, and now she was hurting Barbara. She had every right to dine with Nicholas, she told herself; she shouldn't care if Barbara felt betrayed. But she did care, intensely. The contradiction made her heart pound.

BARBARA STARED INTO the green depths of her tea. Her hand trembled as she lowered the tiny glass, which rattled against the copper tray. She imagined Nicholas's mouth covering Liuba's. Liuba's pale fingers tangled in the darkness of his hair. So they were neither of them mine, and I am to lose them both. I have always been alone.

Or can I hold on to them?

Barbara thought of the ambrotype she'd found at Vanves with Liuba. It was a photograph of a girl and her father. It was very old, printed on glass. The girl's nose was missing and a corner of the father's forehead was gone. She'd bought it anyway, or perhaps because of this. She'd turned it over and discovered two bare patches, where the black paint on the back of the glass was scraped away. Where there was no paint on the back no image appeared on the opposite side. She'd painted over these tiny areas of bareness. Had it worked? She'd turned the ambrotype over and examined the image. The girl's nose had reappeared, as if by magic. The father's forehead was restored.

But can I prevent Nicholas and Liuba from slipping away? Barbara asked herself. "I'm going home," she said calmly. She took out her wallet and paid for both the teas.

"Please stay."

"I have nothing to say. I'd rather be by myself."

"Please stay because I have something to say to you. I am going out to dinner with your brother. But I don't know him, or what I think of him or feel for him. Please don't leave yet."

"Usually it's you who leaves, isn't it?"

"Yes. That's true."

"I'll call you."

THE COURTYARD OUTSIDE the mosque was empty. It was pretty, triangular and white. Barbara crossed through its brief serenity. An arched doorway propelled her into the frantic noise of the city. She looked over her shoulder, but Liuba had not followed her. The Métro carried her home.

There was no sign of the concierge. He was keeping to himself these days. She opened her apartment door. The novelty of fresh paint greeted her. In her bedroom, George sat on her cushion on the floor. She looked at Barbara through sceptical eyes. Sarah and Delphine were occupied with one another.

"Nothing lasts, George. So, why must I?" Barbara went into the living room and tore a strip from the old sheet she'd thrown over the table and chairs while painting.

First she bound George's ankles with the strip of sheet. Round and around went the cloth. George's calves disappeared, and her thighs. Her chest followed. When only George's round wooden head remained visible, Barbara gazed at the pretty red mouth that couldn't quite smile, the blushing cheeks and small, sober eyes.

"I am preserving you," she explained. She made her voice

gentle. She could at least offer George a little tenderness. It was a gift to herself as well. "Don't be frightened. You will last a long time, longer than I will. You are already older than Mémère. You are made of wood and suffer differently."

Thirty-Nine

EUGÉNIE HAD DROPPED HER KNITTING and closed her eyes, when the eyes of a boy named Dimitri confronted her. Why him? she wondered. Why must I remember him? He had come to stay, for a week, when she was seven. He had come with his parents. Everyone called him Dimi. He spoke infrequently, and moved his limbs with a slowness she'd never seen in a boy. But his eyes were not slow. They raced from the mantel, to the bookshelves, to the door and out, and down the path. The pupils were black, and they shrank when he stepped from the darkness of the house into the bright garden. The iris surrounding each black pupil was green, with brown chasms running out to the rim.

"He so loves animals," his mother said.

Dimi allowed Eugénie to follow him down the path to the end of the garden, where he showed her a small guillotine he'd set up. The blade of the penknife was attached to a block of wood. Dimi took a grasshopper from the jar he'd hidden behind some stones and beheaded the innocent insect for her. That was the day that Eugénie understood that adults were blind, and that parents did not know their children. Doubtless they chose not to know them.

THE TELEPHONE RANG. Eugénie opened her eyes. She pulled herself from Mitterrand's cheerful blue embrace and walked towards the ringing.

"*Allô?*"
"Mémère. *C'est moi.* I can't bear it any longer."
"Can't bear what, *ma petite?*"
"Everything."
"I will come to you."
"No, Mémère. It's too far. And mostly I am confused."
"About what?"
"I will tell you another time."
"Shouldn't I come?"
"No."
"What will you do if I don't come?"
"I'll finish painting my apartment. I promise."
"And in an hour I will call and see if you are done?"
"Yes, Mémère. You may call me."

AGAIN EUGÉNIE RESTED her head against Mitterrand's softness. There was another Dimitri, in Kiev. Not the boy who had come to stay and discovered the decisive powers of a guillotine. This other Dimitri had pale eyes.

"Dimitri wears his hat askew, Dimitri's brains are very few, Dimitri smells, peeyew." Son of a tanner. He picked his nose in public. A skin of dried mud coated his shoes.

Shoes should not be muddy. "Eugénie, a young lady keeps both her soul and her shoes clean," instructed her Swiss nanny. She loved this stern woman more than her own mother and had followed her about until the nanny pinned Eugénie to her skirts.

Once Eugénie chanced upon the tanner's son. What was she doing out in the street, alone? He uncurled his grubby fingers to reveal two glossy chestnuts balanced on his palm. What was he offering her? She ran away.

Forgive us our cruelty, thought Eugénie, opening her eyes. She picked up her knitting, and slipped the tip of the needle into the loop of wool. She looked up at the clock. In ten minutes it will be time for me to call Barbara.

Forty

"IT WON'T EVER HAPPEN AGAIN. If I could undo what I've done, I would. He's not in love with me," said Mary. Her hand trembled as she set down the tiny glass of mint tea and the glass knocked against the brass tray.

Rose fished for her wallet. She put money on the table for both their teas and stood up.

"You're leaving? May I call you?" asked Mary.

"I don't know."

"I can pay for my tea."

"What does it matter?"

Mary got up. She followed Rose past the counter displaying sugar-powdered squares of Turkish delight and curled sweets bathing in honey, and out into the heat of the triangular, white courtyard. They continued through the arched doorway and onto the sidewalk in front of the mosque.

"Please," said Rose turning to face Mary, "leave me alone."

Mary watched as Rose crossed the street and entered the Jardin des Plantes. I mustn't follow. But if I don't, I'll never see her again. The words pulsated in her mind with an unknowable certainty, as if they'd travelled backwards to her from the future. She ran across the street and through the gates. She caught up with Rose, the gravel path crunching under her sandals in the silence of the gardens. They walked beside each other, beneath the plane trees, past the pink roses. They said nothing under the pruned branches and the untrimmed blue of the summer sky.

Outside the lower gates, in the whorl of indifferent movement of pedestrians navigating past each other along hot sidewalks, Rose stopped walking.

"Shouldn't I be happy it's over? He wasn't going to stay. Now I'm free."

The light turned green and Rose crossed the boulevard, Mary hurrying beside her.

"You aren't going to stay either," said Rose. "Only I'll stay. But maybe I won't. I'll be free too."

"What about Nicholas and Barbara? And Mémère?"

"You're right. I'm not free, or alone. But they would be better free of me, my children. That's how I feel at times. I would like to know how to fly. Would you?"

"Fly?"

"Yes. When I was a child, the most daring boys used to balance on the walls along the quays. Shall we try?"

"No. I'm afraid of heights," said Mary.

They were halfway across the Pont d'Austerlitz. Rose took off her shoes and she climbed onto the wall of the bridge.

"There. What did I tell you? I am free as a bird. I'm never going to fall in love again. I will love only my children and my mother." She walked along the broad wall, her naked toes holding the stone, her arms outstretched.

Mary picked up Rose's sandals and walked beside her, on the sidewalk. A man and a woman were crossing the bridge from the other direction. They watched Rose.

"Please come down," said Mary. But she didn't have the right to ask anything more of Rose. How faint her words sounded against the hot expanse of the sky.

Where did the breeze come from? Mary had hoped all day for some small movement in the air. Now a sultry gust picked itself up, rushed through the blue stillness and grabbed Rose's straw hat. Rose's hand and her small cry flew up together. Her arms flailed as she dropped over the edge.

    Mary saw Rose strike the surface of the water. There was a great splash. Rose's dark head, small now, surfaced. Her head moved through the waves, in the direction of the bank. Then the river tugged harder and the dark head disappeared.

    Mary leaned still farther out over the wall, her eyes searching the suddenly choppy surface of the water. The river continued on its way, as if it carried no one buried inside it.

    Mary felt her head grow light. Next, a hand slapped her cheek. The woman who'd been crossing the bridge with her husband was kneeling beside her. The man had run for help. Mary stared at Rose's sandals. They lay on the sidewalk where they'd fallen from her hand.

Forty-One

TIME RESEMBLED A WINGED INSECT. One moment it flew, the next it crawled. In three days' time, thought Nicholas, I will dine with a woman named love. Though he did not speak Russian, he knew the word for love was "liubov." The significance of a chance word, he reflected, must never be underestimated. He laughed, and in a recess of his mind he heard Anna also laughing at his silliness. Then he brushed his teeth.

In his dream that night, he swam in a cast-iron cauldron. Round and round he paddled, dodging the wooden spoons. They were gathered around the rim of the cauldron, peering down—Rose, Mémère, Barbara, Anna, Janine. They tossed in sweet basil, lizards' tongues, sage and thyme, frogs' legs, milk, and honey. This way and that he swam, the liquid growing hotter, sucking him under, the great wooden spoons mixing, churning. Above him, above the rim, the women sang.

He woke, flailing his arms, kicking at the covers. Sitting up, he drank from the glass of water beside his bed. Sunday. He had to wait three more days before seeing Liuba. Would she be as he remembered?

IN THE MIDDLE of the morning, Eugénie telephoned.
"Can you come for coffee at three o'clock? Are you free, *mon petit?*"
"Today?"
"Yes. I couldn't ask you sooner, because I only found out today."
"Found out what?"
"I will explain once you are here."
"You can't tell me over the telephone?"
"I have never liked telephones."
"*Ah bon?*"
"They have their uses."
"Is it urgent? You're not unwell?"
"I am as well as can be expected. So, I will see you?"
There was nothing to be gained by arguing with Mémère.
"Yes. You will see me. At three o'clock, you will have the dubious pleasure of my company."

HE GOT INTO HIS CAR at the appointed hour and drove across the city. They were waiting for him. Not only Mémère, but Claire and Léon.
"*Bonjour,*" said Claire. "Maman, I will make the coffee."
A plate of plain cookies, a bowl of oranges, and a chocolate cake sat on the table in the round dining room.
"It is because of Barbara," Eugénie announced. He hadn't yet taken off his raincoat. "She has fallen."
"From where?" He decided to keep his coat on. He stood in front of the windows.
"Yesterday, she climbed her stepladder to finish painting her bedroom. Someone knocked at her door, possibly her concierge. The knock startled her and she lost her balance," explained Eugénie.
"Did she break anything?"
"Her left arm and wrist," interjected Léon, selecting a

cookie. "Barbara is fine, but Mémère is under the impression that this fall signifies something else. A loss of stability? *N'est-ce pas*, Mémère? We are here to reassure you, Mémère, that Barbara is an adult with a broken arm, and otherwise in good health."

"Her arm and wrist, nothing worse? Then I will take off my coat," said Nicholas.

"Barbara says that now she will not get married," said Claire.

"She was never serious about this Henri," said Nicholas. "Her injury is an excuse to be rid of him."

"Possibly Barbara is frightened," suggested Claire.

"Yes. But of what?" asked Nicholas. He ground a crumb into the tablecloth with his thumb.

"There is a lot in the world that is frightening," commented Léon. "You must encounter fear in your patients all the time, Nicholas. Yet in your sister it irritates you." Léon had hoped to spend the afternoon quietly reading.

"I'm not my sister's doctor," answered Nicholas. "There is nothing surprising in my lack of patience with her."

"Happily, they are only broken bones. They'll mend. Perhaps when the shock of falling has passed, she will patch things up with Henri," suggested Claire. "Or, possibly, their marriage was not meant to be. One is so vulnerable when living alone. The fall may have made her acutely aware of her isolation. The sort of inner isolation, a refusal to accept one's true self, that marriage cannot cure. Perhaps when she's stronger she will marry him." Claire glanced at her mother.

Eugénie, slumped in her chair, was sleeping.

"It is possible that Henri does not exist," proposed Nicholas. Some time ago he'd begun toying with the idea that Henri might be a fantasy. Although the idea made no sense, it intrigued him, and now it had slipped out. "It is only an impression that comes to me fleetingly," he explained. "Has either of you met Henri?" He paused. He received no answer. He was enjoying himself. "I've never met Henri, though not from lack of trying. Why has Barbara been determined to repaint her apartment if she was intending to marry and move out?"

"She may never have intended to marry him, despite what she told us. But how does that suggest that Henri doesn't exist? You don't believe she's mad, do you?" said Léon. "Surely she has a right to her privacy."

"But, of course, Léon, she has a right to her privacy." Nicholas leaned back in his chair. "Henri is such a private matter that she complains about him to Mémère endlessly. Yet he never appears in flesh and blood. Business commitments detain him abroad. Have you met him?"

"No, I haven't." Léon cracked open the shell of a walnut.

"Léon, Maman is sleeping," said Claire and laid her hand on his arm.

"We are practically shouting at one another and have failed to wake her. I doubt my cracking a walnut will disturb her," replied Léon, removing Claire's hand with gentle firmness. "She has the right to wake up, if she wants to. This is her dining room." With the tip of his dessert fork, he dislodged a section of the nut.

"I haven't met Henri," said Claire, smoothing the tablecloth. She felt certain Nicholas was teasing but the idea intrigued her. "I've attributed Barbara's secretiveness to a fear of how we might judge him. She must sense how curious we are." What would Rose have made of all this? Claire wondered.

"Suppose that this man we are calling Henri does not exist. Then Barbara is mad. Is that what you are suggesting, Nicholas?" asked Léon.

"Barbara is infuriating but not mad. Henri's non-existence is my own fantasy," said Nicholas, stretching his arms above his head. "I should never have mentioned it," he reprimanded himself aloud. Henri exists, yes, but not as far as Barbara is concerned. I'm sure she doesn't allow him to exist.

He sat down and peeled an orange. He arranged the bright sections in a circle on his plate.

"965. I'm listening." The young telephone operator had stopped coming to her appointments. He'd moved a psychotic shoe salesman into her time slot. The poor man was gripped by intolerable anxiety at the sight of an uneven number. He had been apprehended while defacing the licence plate of a neighbour's car, scratching off the uneven numbers with a nail. Metal scraping metal. That was the sound of the man's dreams as they'd tumbled out of him. While listening, Nicholas had held on to the image of the licence plate, to its redemptive absurdity. But the salesman's pain had cut and scraped its way into his being all the same.

"Nicholas," said Claire, "if Henri does not exist I can understand, I think, why Barbara invented him."

"Claire, Claire. It's not Barbara but you who's mad," protested Léon. "I'll invite Henri to lunch."

"And I promise you he won't come," said Nicholas.

"Of course he won't. Because Barbara has broken his heart," said Léon.

Three sharp rings announced someone on the telephone. Eugénie opened her eyes and grabbed the edge of the table.

"Don't move," commanded Nicholas.

"There's no rush, Maman," added Claire. "Léon is answering it."

"Barbara," said Léon into the receiver. "How are you? Of course Mémère is here. I will pass you to her."

Forty-Two

ANNA WAS NOT READING HER BOOK. How could she, with all of them in there, sipping their coffee? Do they know I'm in my room? Does Nicholas care? What is he saying? What is he doing with his hands?

Anna had heard them arrive. First Léon and Claire and, ten minutes later, Nicholas. Barbara had not come. Why?

Anna closed her book. I will tell him I love him, she resolved. And he'll say, "I would make you miserable," but what he'll really mean is that I would make him miserable. Then it'll all be over. The blade will fall and darkness will swallow me.

Anna walked down the narrow hall. In her hands, she clutched her essay, "Balzac and the Demons of Progress." Could they hear her heart, beating wildly as she approached? How dangerous, to have one's heart beat so loudly because of another person. Her heart's thumping filled her ears.

"Ah, Anna," said Léon.

"Anna, come in," invited Eugénie. "There is plenty of cake and some cookies left. And we have finished our serious meeting, or rather my family talked while I slept."

"Thank you, Mémère, but I'm not hungry. I've come to ask a favour . . . a question. . . ." Anna stared across the room. In

Nicholas's left hand lay a curl of orange peel. She looked down at her ugly shoes, then fixed her attention on the blue Moroccan bowl resting on the sideboard. A tightrope walker, she told herself, must fix her gaze ahead, allow no wavering. "It's about grammar," she hurried on. "There's something I don't understand. I must hand in my paper, and..." She held out her essay.

"But of course. Let me see," said Léon.

It hadn't occurred to her that someone other than Nicholas might offer to help. She hadn't thought her plan through. How could she have been so stupid? She walked past Léon without answering him and stood beside Nicholas's chair. It didn't matter if she hurt Léon's feelings. Soon it would all be over.

"Please, I must speak with you."

Nicholas stood up. "I'm going to take the Cadillac to the kitchen; will you come along and help me unload it?" he said. "I'd be happy to look at your paper. I expect there won't be much for me to correct."

"Thank you," she said.

They left the dining room together, the metal wheels of Eugénie's trolley squeaking in front of them. Nicholas parked the noisy vehicle and closed the kitchen door.

"There. No one will disturb us," he said.

Anna looked out the kitchen window. The courtyard formed a grey pit, a deep cage, a contained drabness. Did every building in Paris hold such an ugly space at its centre? Nicholas stood behind her, waiting for her to speak, to hand him her paper, and ask about the rules of grammar.

"I love you," she said, looking down into the grey yard where the residents' garbage waited in bins to be taken away. The clock ticked on the wall. Bread crusts waited in the cloth bag suspended from the door handle. Jam sat in jars, and plums swam in their vinegar baths. "I love you," she repeated.

"I would make you miserable, Anna."

But he didn't say it the way he was meant to, with gallant courtesy. She hadn't expected him to sound regretful.

"I work all the time. There's no poetry in me, only doubt and ambition. I stare at ugliness and pick it apart. You would find me very boring." He spoke with conviction. But what he was saying wasn't true. It's not me you're rejecting, decided Anna, but a part of yourself. You coward. She turned and faced him. She wanted to shove him against the stove and beat him with her fists.

"How do you know what I'd feel?" she asked.

"I don't."

"Then it's yourself you're talking about. You love me but you're a coward."

She ran from the kitchen, down the bare corridor to her room and lay on her bed and cried. On the faded blue silk of the wall danced a fragile light. It slipped through the tall windows, between the candy-striped curtains that reached to the floor.

Forty-Three

Barbara stood the bouquets of flowers on the floor and counted them. Three bouquets were held in vases, four in old jars. Mimosa, cornflowers, daisies, roses, lilies. Nicholas, Mémère, Léon and Claire, Liuba, even Anna, Madame Couchon from downstairs, everyone at work.

They think I've died, or why send so many flowers? How simple that would make things for them, to have me disappear for good. Look at all these blossoms. Their true purpose is to celebrate my death.

Barbara lay down on her back, fitting herself into the narrow space between the vessels of flowers. To the left of her nose spread a pink lily, its stamen heavy with pollen. Beside her chin exploded the pure blue of a cornflower. Carnations made red declarations above her knees. She turned her head and studied the thorns on the stems of the roses. Her broken arm, encased in heavy plaster, rested beside her.

"I'm not going to marry you, Henri. I'm sorry," she told her absent lover.

"Is there someone else?" he asked.

"Only me. I'm the other person."

The mingling perfumes, the light passing through the coloured petals. So much beauty at a funeral?

Perhaps they don't think I've died, Nicholas and Liuba, Mémère, Claire and Léon. Is it possible that they love me?

And Anna? No. Anna doesn't love me. She can't have forgiven me for what I said about her mother. Why should she forgive me? Her daisies are politeness.

And Liuba's roses? She'll fall in love with Nicholas. Women always do.

Nicholas's lilies? What sort of resurrection is he hoping for? When did he start to avoid me? When I was six? Seven?

Barbara breathed slowly. She rode on a carpet of colours and scents, out of the room, across the city, above its rooftops. She opened her eyes. She was lying in her own white living room surrounded by flowers, the air thick with their mingled perfumes.

She sat up. I will quit the Samaritaine, she told herself. I will take my folder of drawings and look for work. I'll make costumes large enough for people to wear. I'll help people disguise themselves in beauty or ugliness.

She sat alert, surrounded by flowers, and planned her future. Yes, it occurred to her. Perhaps they love me.

Forty-Four

THE MOZART SONATA CAME TO AN END. Eugénie and Claire, embraced by Mitterrand, listened to the plumber in the apartment below hammer on pipes. Two days had passed since the family "council."

"Barbara wouldn't have fallen if I had paid more attention to her," said Eugénie.

"What more could you have done, Maman? You couldn't very well have stood at the base of her ladder waiting to catch her."

"My thinking was wrong." Eugénie smoothed the material of her skirt.

"Maman, you'll tire yourself, thinking this way. It's only her arm and wrist, and they will mend."

"Yes. I am tired. I have not yet learned enough, and so God is keeping me alive. He's keeping me alive until I am wiser. But I would like to rest."

"Maman, let me fix you a tisane."

"I wasn't able to save Rose."

"Nor was I. But she wasn't a little girl. When we were little, Maman, you did everything you could for us."

"No. It was the two of you who looked after me."

"Maman, why don't you lie down? I'll go into the next room and read until you wake up."

"Yes. I will go and lie down. I am tired."

"Let me take your arm."

"No. Thank you. I will go on my own."

"Maman, none of us was of enough help to Rose. That was a long time ago."

"It was only a short while ago. Don't wait for me to finish my nap. Go home to Léon. He needs you."

"Will you call me later this evening?" Claire took her mother's hand and held it in her own. Condensed, concentrated, you no longer fill your skin, Maman. Age has distilled you. How loosely your skin fits over your bones.

Forty-Five

MARKET STALLS LINED THE RUE DE SEINE, selling fruit, flowers, and plucked chickens dangling by their scrawny necks. For the length of one block no cars were permitted.

Anna stopped at the first vegetable stand. It was a sunny day. Behind her, across the street, three tables and six chairs with woven plastic seats were set on the terrace of the Café du Marche.

Someone was watching her. This wasn't the first time she'd felt the enquiry of his eyes. From her position of safety, close to the aubergines and cauliflowers, she studied him. He sat, legs crossed at the ankles, large feet. He had a high forehead, which was baking in the spring sunshine. His battered blue bicycle leaned chained to a lamppost. Last week she'd seen him arrive on the bicycle, surprisingly graceful and silent. Would a murderer ride a bicycle? She didn't think so.

THE CUSTOMER AHEAD of Anna was being served from the orderly pyramids of aubergines. Anna removed the clip from her hair and rearranged it so that no strand tugged painfully. She fished in her bag. But for what? Her fingers touched a pen and her notebook. She extracted these, then dropped them in again. She turned and looked across the street. His eyes were too far away for her to see into them. For the past three Tuesdays, this blind touching with their eyes, this exchange had gone on between them.

"*Et pour mademoiselle?*" asked the grocer.

"I don't know yet. I'm so sorry."

"You are too pretty to be sorry."

"I'll have two tomatoes and a cauliflower, *s'il vous plait.*"

ANNA CROSSED THE STREET, her book bag hanging from her shoulder, her sack of vegetables dangling from her hand. She stopped in front of the man.

"My name is Anna." She freed her right hand and held it out. He took her hand in his. His skin felt dry and warm. He had long fingers.

"And my name is Gerrard. Won't you sit down?"

He released her hand and she sat, her bag of books filling her lap. His eyes were brown, calm on the surface.

"Is that your bicycle?" she asked.

"Yes, that's my bicycle. You've been watching me, but whenever I look over, you look away or pretend to hunt for something in your bag. I was feeling quite annoyed with you." He was smiling. He reached for his glass of beer, but before lifting it, he asked Anna, "Will you have something? I'm glad you've come to speak with me."

"I'll have the same as you are having. Thank you. Have you had your bicycle for a long time?"

"You think it looks beat up? You're right. It's been with me longer than most of my friends."

"My bicycle is old also. I wish I had one here. Mine is at home."

"Where is home?"

"Canada."

The waiter appeared in the doorway in overalls and cap, humming a passage from *Carmen*. Gerrard called him over and ordered two beers.

"I've always wanted to see Canada. You're lucky to have a home. I was born in this city but it's no home unless you're wealthy. One small room is not a home; not when the woman next door is a bitch who pounds on your wall. I hope my language doesn't offend you?"

"It doesn't offend me."

"Some women can't bear to hear a man say anything insulting about any woman. That doesn't stop them from saying horrendous things about one another behind each other's backs." Gerrard's glass stood empty, a tiny row of bubbles sliding down its interior.

The waiter, still humming *Carmen*, placed the beers upon the table.

"The Greek gods," said Gerrard, "they insulted each other. Those are the sort of gods we need. Ones in whose image we could conceivably have been made."

Anna felt him begin his study of her, starting at the part in her hair. His eyes reached her small breasts, hidden beneath her shirt.

She started falling. Now, only his vision of her mattered. She kept falling as his eyes returned to her face.

"Does Greek mythology interest you? What do you like to read?" he asked her.

"I don't want to talk about anything with you. I know a lot of people with whom I can have long conversations."

"Then why did you cross the street and come to my table?"

"I want you to take me to bed."

Gerrard's smile grew. His face opened, surprise and pleasure sweeping in. "That's why you came over?"

"Yes."

"How lovely." He covered her hand with his. "But I must warn you, my room is ugly. Not fit for you. Could we go to your place?"

"You can't come to where I live. That's impossible. I don't care if your room is ugly."

"We have no reason to stay here. Don't you agree?"

"Yes, I agree."

Gerrard stood up. "I live rather far away. But we can walk. Do you mind a bit of a walk?"

"I love to walk."

Anna waited while he unchained his bicycle. They didn't speak until they reached the Seine. She learned that he had worked painting and building theatre sets, that he was at present unemployed, that most afternoons he cycled to the Café du Marche, drank and watched women buying their vegetables, their chickens, and their cheese in the marketplace.

They followed the river and crossed on the Pont d'Austerlitz. They walked up l'avenue Ledru Rollin, where Gerrard stopped and locked his bicycle to a post. The street was lined with thick, old plane trees. He opened a heavy green door and they climbed five flights of stairs.

A long time ago someone had painted the room mauve. A chipped enamelled table stood in one corner. On the floor, two cartons of books. A large brown stain in the shape of a boot spread from the ceiling down the wall. "It looks like Italy. That stain. Don't you think?" he said. "That's where my mother came from, Italy. So I suppose I'm fated to be stuck in this room."

While he unbuttoned her shirt, Anna examined the shape of Italy. When he touched her naked breasts, she discovered that they were made to be touched.

AFTERWARDS, ANNA LAY on her side, linked to all the people outside in the street who went to their rooms and made love, who were made either less lonely or lonelier by this act.

Gerrard sat up and scratched his back.

"Gerrard," she said, experimenting, listening to his name. "I'm sorry about your sheet."

"You think I care about my sheet? You are what matters." He crouched beside her and kissed her. That, she thought, felt delicious.

"Would you like some of this?" he asked, crossing his room and picking up a bottle half-full of wine that stood on the enamelled table. "I'd make you a coffee but I used up my last this morning."

"I'll have some wine. Thank you."

He found a clean glass. As a precaution, he wiped it with the corner of his tea towel, his fingers moving inside the cloth. He filled the glass and handed it to her. "Did I give you any pleasure?" he asked.

"Yes. Thank you."

"It will get better."

"Do you think so?"

"I hope so. I'll do my best."

She drank the wine, saying his name inside her head, while he lay on his back beside her and smoked a cigarette.

Forty-Six

Today, the telephone held no power over Eugénie Balashovskaya. She didn't care if it stopped ringing before her arrival. She walked, looking down at the intricate pattern of colours passing slowly under her feet. She picked up the receiver.

"Mémère?"

"*Oui, ma petite?*"

"I have given notice at the Samaritaine."

"And what will you do?"

"I'll send out my drawings."

"Ah, Barbara, *je te félicite*. Your drawings are very good. You have talent and you are hardworking. It will not be easy but you will succeed. This is what I have been hoping for."

Relief spread through Eugénie. She looked about her. The apartment did not feel as empty as it had earlier. A sunny breeze was coming in from the balcony, and the plants were growing.

Forty-Seven

THE DOORS OF THE PAVILLON MONTSOURIS stood open and tables were set on the terrace. The trees were dressed in their new leaves. The tenderness of evening invaded the park. Liuba ordered snails and Nicholas chose a rooster's crest.

"There's something I must tell you," said Liuba as she unfolded her napkin. She'd vowed to herself to speak without delay.

"Should I be frightened?" asked Nicholas.

"No."

"Then tell me."

"Your sister Barbara and I are friends. We met in February. We see a good deal of each other."

Nicholas studied her dark eyes, her wide and somewhat awkward mouth. He wanted to say too much at once, and so he said nothing. Not far off, hidden in the whispering foliage, a cardinal sang. A twig snapped.

"You're a friend of Barbara's," he repeated at last.

"Yes. I should have told you the day we met."

"And why didn't you?"

"I was enjoying listening to your stories and I was afraid you'd stop."

"You knew everything already."

"Not from your point of view."

Nicholas picked up his fork, twirled it between his fingers and put it down. He laughed. "So there's no escaping my sister. She'll pursue me forever." He studied Liuba's face. "I don't know what to tell you, because you may have heard the opposite."

"I have something else to confess to you," said Liuba. Her snails had arrived. She stabbed one and ate it. She twisted her ring around her finger.

"There's more?" said Nicholas.

"Yes. I don't feel I have a right to be here, eating dinner with you. It feels disloyal. Although that doesn't make any sense. You're not your sister's lover."

"No, I'm certainly not."

"But I feel I'm betraying her, that I'm repeating the past."

"What past? The past is big."

"Your mother, Sherbatsky and Mary."

"She told you all that? Of course she would."

"I want to be here." Liuba smiled at him. She ate a snail. "These are delicious. But am I betraying Barbara? How much loyalty should a person offer to a friend? I can't decide."

"In my opinion, you have every right to eat dinner with me. As for the past, it's not certain my mother was betrayed by Mary Bertram. My father, on the other hand, did behave horribly towards my mother. That's certain."

"Barbara seems more concerned about Mary and Sherbatsky than about your father."

"No doubt she has her reasons. Just as I have had my reasons to defend Mary." Nicholas took a piece of bread. He spread the butter carefully to the edges. *It was the fault of the rain.* He saw in his memory the tiny sketch of the llama's head. He pictured Sherbatsky's fingers touching the nape of Mary's neck, as she bent to adjust her shoe. Barbara had described it to him more than once. He bit his piece of buttered bread.

"I was fond of Mary. Very fond of her. And I haven't wanted

to believe that my mother suffered two grave disappointments in a row. I also have had cause not to trust every word my sister tells me. She has a rich imagination and is given to jealousy; or perhaps that's not how she seems to you?"

"Yes. She's a bit jealous, and certainly imaginative." I'm already betraying her, thought Liuba.

The waiter brought Liuba her perch, and Nicholas his guinea fowl. She peeled back the flesh of the fish and removed its spine. Nicholas watched the careful movement of her fine wrist as she deposited the spine on the side of her plate.

"Must your sense of loyalty to my sister prevent you from getting to know me a bit better?"

"I'm not sure. I guess I'll find out."

He filled her glass with wine. He cut a piece from the bird on his plate and ate it.

Darkness filled the park. A first star pricked the sky above the trees. As they consumed their main courses, Nicholas asked Liuba about her childhood. He didn't want to miss the beginning. He braided the episodes and began his ascent to the tower window, curious to press his lips to her wide mouth, to cradle her breasts in his hands.

Forty-Eight

Though the room felt chilly, Anna did not close the window. She stood, watching the rain darken the trunks of the old trees. She wrapped the sheet she'd pulled from the bed higher around her naked shoulders.

"I like being in your room," she said, and smiled at Gerrard.

"And me? Do you like me?" he asked. He was lying on his back, exposed. He didn't seem bothered by the chilly air.

She had no answer to offer him. He was asking her for more than she could give.

"If you like me," continued Gerrard, propping himself on his elbow, studying her across his room, "why won't you tell me where you live? I wouldn't have to stay the night. You could make me a cup of tea, then send me away. Not even that. All you say is that it's in the Sixteenth Arrondissement and very fancy. Are you afraid I won't behave? Is it your old Russian landlady? Are you scared she'll tell your mother you're fucking some guy you met in a café?"

"She wouldn't tell. She wouldn't know, and if she did, she wouldn't tell."

"So you just don't want me around?"

In answer, Anna crossed the room. She rested her cheek on his stomach.

"I don't really give a shit about your old Russian and anyone else who lives in the Sixteenth. They all have rods stuck up their asses."

She didn't try to stop him from insulting Mémère, Nicholas, and Claire. He didn't matter, not enough to argue with. With each breath he took, her head rose and fell on his warm, taut, stomach,

"Will you bring me to your log cabin in Canada? I'd rather go there than to the Sixteenth Arrondissement. I won't mind the snow; I'll learn how to trap furs." He ran his fingers through her hair. She examined a muscle that led to his elbow. At his elbow, it stopped and another one started on its way to his shoulder.

"I'll buy myself a pair of snowshoes. Or you can offer me a pair for a present."

"How do you support yourself, here in Paris, where you can't trap animals for their furs?"

"Do you think I steal?"

"No."

"When my father died last year, he left me his savings. That's what enables me to survive. When that's gone, I'll look for work again." His finger slipped down the side of her neck.

She lifted her head, placed her mouth over his and kissed him. If I don't love you, she thought, the least I can do is kiss you. That much I can offer, and take. I owe you for putting an end to my awful innocence and to a portion of my fears.

"I have worked, you know," he said. "I've loaded up trucks with useless boxes and painted theatre sets for people who spent all their time arguing. I've cooked in filthy kitchens."

Anna made a disgusted face.

"Is that face for me?"

"No, for the kitchens. The awful places you've had to work."

"You're not going to get all wound up, judging me? Or pitying me?"

Her breasts hung above his chest. He reached up, and rolled the pink nipples between his thumbs and fingers.

"I LIKE THE WARMTH of your skin," said Anna, later. She stroked his penis, and it nudged her hand, asking for more. She watched it grow, reminded of a film she'd seen that showed fiddleheads uncurling in slow motion. His penis was also a divining rod, bending towards the liquids inside her.

Why don't I love you? Because you feel sorry for yourself. You expect cruelty and hand it out ahead of time. You probably weren't loved as a child, and I can't do anything about that. If I loved you, I'd imagine healing you. But I don't love you and Nicholas doesn't love me. Around and around it goes. But it isn't futile. It mustn't be. Anna kissed his closed eyelids.

WHILE GERRARD PREPARED their lunch on the chipped, enamelled table, Anna sat cross-legged on his mattress, her head resting against the wall.

"Only a handful of people on the planet know how to prepare a proper salad dressing," Gerrard said. He held an avocado and a knife. "Most people use the wrong proportions." Anna was relieved that his hands were occupied with something other than her. She watched his hand cut the avocado in half, the shadow of his action thrown against the mauve wall.

"A friend of mine is coming by. I've told him about you, and he's eager to meet you," said Gerrard.

"Who is he?"

"His name is Jean. Lunch is served."

She watched him dry his hands on a dish towel, then she got up and came to the table. As she stood beside the table, he wrapped the dish towel around her waist and pulled her tight against him. His lips explored her neck; the liquid muscle of his tongue penetrated her ear.

"When is your friend coming?" she asked, when he'd finished with her ear.

"In about half an hour, if he's on time. Does it matter? Are you afraid he'll eat your share of the lunch?" Gerrard stabbed a slice of purple onion with his fork.

"What does your friend do?"

"What does my friend do?" asked Gerrard, mimicking Anna's accent. "His name is Jean. I told you his name. You can call him by his name. That would be more polite. He builds theatre sets. Does that meet with your approval?"

"Why wouldn't I approve of Jean? I love the theatre." She wiped the corner of her mouth with her napkin.

"This is delicious," she said. "Thank you."

"Good. I'm glad you like it. But you don't know anything about theatres. You have no idea the nastiness that goes on there, the back-stabbing. I wouldn't let you anywhere near one."

Anna felt tired of his tedious jabbings. Her purse lay where she'd dropped it on his mattress. She got up from the table, walked over to the mattress, and pulled from the little bag a silver tube of lipstick. She crawled across the mattress to where a round, unframed mirror hung low on the wall, and applied the colour to her lips.

"This is the first time I've seen you wear lipstick," Gerrard remarked, his tone sharpening against some hidden stone, sending off sparks. He was holding his fork and knife in his hands. You should be clutching lightning bolts, like one of your Greek gods, thought Anna.

"I don't often wear lipstick," she said. "That's true."

"You couldn't be bothered to paint your lips for me, but for Jean . . ."

Anna smiled. She teetered on the edge of laughter, startled by his silly jealousy, incredulous. But she caught herself and didn't laugh.

"You're preparing yourself for him," he accused her.

"I don't know him."

"Precisely. You don't have to."

"I don't care about Jean."

"That's my point. For you, anyone will do."

"You're jealous," she said. It was remarkable that she had made a man jealous, and without wanting to or trying. She forgot, for a moment, to feel frightened of his mounting anger. "Gerrard," she could have said, "you have no idea what sort of person I am." But she couldn't be bothered telling him what he should have understood for himself.

"You're behaving like a whore."

"I put on lipstick for your friend."

"You never pretty yourself up for me." His breathing quickened.

"I'm going home. Please tell your friend I'm sorry but I couldn't stay."

"I don't want you to stay."

Now she heard the hatred in his voice. It travelled through her in swift, chopping waves. When confronted with an unwell animal, Anna thought, it is best not to move suddenly. She picked up her purse and crossed the room, slowly, to the door. Gerrard stood in silence, still clutching his cutlery. She opened the door, stepped through, and closed it behind her. The stairs disappeared under her feet two at a time. He did not follow.

She walked past his chained bicycle and on, beneath the old plane trees. The rain had ended. At the end of his street, the trees stopped. She continued along the sidewalk, stepping around the puddles. By the time she reached the Pont d'Austerlitz, she decided he would not follow.

The river formed an opening and the grey sky rolled out wide above her. A flight of stairs led down to the Seine. She started her descent. He doesn't know my telephone number, or my address, she thought. He could wait outside the Sorbonne, but there would be lots of people around.

She walked along the cobblestones and sat down on a wet bench beneath a poplar tree. The poplar's leaves trembled, whispering to each other. She pulled out of her purse the little red address book she'd stolen from her mother. "It was the fault of the rain. No, it was my fault. I can't blame the rain." The leaves went on whispering to each other.

Forty-Nine

Anna heard Eugénie's shuffling feet approach along the bare corridor. Next, a rapping against the door.

"Come in," Anna called, sitting up and smoothing the green bedspread.

A strand of Eugénie's black hair had slipped from its pins. It dangled beside her cheek. She brushed the hairs away from her skin, with her left hand. In her right hand she held a small plate.

"Forgive me for disturbing you so late in the evening, Anna. But have you had your dessert yet?"

"No, I haven't, Mémère."

"Then take this piece of tart. Last night Nicholas came to dinner. He didn't eat a great deal."

"Thank you. Plum is my favourite. Won't you come in?"

"No, thank you. I am on my way to bed. I am tired." But Eugénie remained in the doorway, and allowed herself to lean against the door frame. "Did you know I spoke Italian?" she asked.

"No. You never told me."

" *'Ma come mi sono ridotta?'* That's the only sentence I know."

"What does it mean?"

"How have I fallen so low?"

"Won't you come in and sit down, Mémère? Where did you learn Italian?"

"If I allow myself to sit, I won't have the energy to get up again. The tale of my Italian sentence is brief, a tale I can tell while standing."

"The tale of your only sentence?"

"When Nicholas was twelve, he and a friend took me to see an Italian film. I have forgotten who the director was. I forget everything these days. There were many naked women in the film, and Nicholas and his friend had invited me so they might see how I would react. One of these women, though she was married, went to bed with a man who was not her husband. First she cried, and then she shouted *'Ma come mi sono ridotta?'* 'How have I fallen so low?' And then she cried some more and shouted again, *'Ma come mi sono ridotta?'*"

"How did you react?"

Eugénie laughed. "I loved the sound of that woman's voice, and I decided to learn Italian. I learned one sentence."

"What about the army and going to Italy? Nicholas claims you joined the army at the end of the war and were stationed in Italy as a translator?"

"Ah, yes. That is true. But *that* Italian I've forgotten." A thorny vine of pain was climbing Eugénie's leg. She wriggled her foot, but the agony had rooted itself between her toes. "When you have eaten the tart, please return my plate to me. Over the years everyone has broken my dessert plates. I have only two of this design left."

"Yes, Mémère. I promise to return your plate. Sleep well."

But Eugénie remained in the doorway. "Sometimes, Anna, someone good falls low and has to live with their guilt. None of us is safe from falling. So who are we to judge?"

Do you mean I've fallen, or is it my mother you're thinking of? wondered Anna. Or the woman in the film? Or yourself?

"Who fell? My mother?"

"Yes. I think Barbara told you. It is likely your mother loved Ivan Sherbatsky. I wish Barbara hadn't said what she did to you. But we all act in ways we regret. Don't judge your mother harshly. It is not up to us to judge one another. But we all do. Good night, *ma petite*. We will speak further in the morning." Eugénie turned her back on Anna, crossed the narrow corridor, and entered her bedroom, closing the door behind her.

Anna shut her own door and leaned against it. She tried to cry but couldn't. She sat in the sunken green chair in front of the tall windows and ate her slice of plum tart. Will she speak to me in the morning? She won't, decided Anna. The moment is gone.

She closed her eyes and saw Rodin's girl with the marble head, hands raised to mouth, a cage of fingers, the open spaces between the fingers.

Fifty

Anna pressed the doorbell. Was he at home? How did he spend his Saturday mornings?

Nicholas opened the door. "*Ah, bonjour,*" he exclaimed. The pleasure in his eyes and his smile gave her confidence.

"I've come to see the painting. Am I disturbing you? You're probably busy. I should have called."

"Come in. I do have to go out. But not quite yet."

She found herself standing in a narrow hall paved with cobblestones. It must have once belonged to an exterior yard.

"*Viens,*" said Nicholas. "I'll show you the portrait."

She followed him along the cobblestones a short distance and entered a small living room. The portrait hung on the wall facing her. Anna would have felt more comfortable had Rose been looking sideways or down at some object in her hands. But no, Rose gazed straight at whoever chanced to enter the room.

The lines were confident, except for a sloppiness around the left ear. The colours were rich, the paint applied with vigour. Yet there was tenderness. Life glimmered, hovered, especially in the quiet eyes and generous mouth. Her dark, abundant hair caught the light. A broad cheekbone cast a mauve shadow. Her blouse was a deep purple and her lips were parted in a smile.

"Did she look like that? Your mother?" asked Anna.

"The look of anxious apology at the back of her eyes, your mother captured that well. And the generosity of her smile. Did my mother look like this painting? I don't remember her in a single image. But this painting hangs here all the time, and sometimes it seems more convincing than my memories of her. What do you think of it? Does it resemble your mother's other work?"

"I can tell it's my mother's. It's one of her best."

"You told me that your mother keeps her paintings hidden on a third floor?"

"Yes. Except for the one in my room. It's of two women playing chess. They haven't any faces."

Anna could feel Rose's grey eyes studying her from the canvas on the wall.

"I'm sorry," she said.

"Sorry for what?"

"For calling you a coward, that day in the kitchen." She felt hot with shame but also brave.

"I have been a coward," said Nicholas. "Although not in the way you believe, perhaps. But cowardly nonetheless. In the last few days, I've become less so. Or so I hope."

"How have you changed?"

"It's complicated."

Anna waited for him to explain, but he didn't speak. "I'm also sorry about my mother." Anna raised her eyes from Nicholas's shoulders to his face. "My mother did sleep with Sherbatsky. You said in the restaurant that you didn't believe she betrayed your mother. But she did. Even Mémère says so."

"Mémère has discussed it with you?"

"Last night. Only briefly. I don't think she will again. She said I should be forgiving."

"And are you?"

"It's not really any of my business. I thought it was. I want to be accepting. I've been rather selfish and cruel to someone, these past few weeks. Mémère used the word 'love.' She said my mother loved Sherbatsky."

"I expect she did."

"That doesn't mean she had any right—" Anna began. She looked straight at Nicholas. The expression in his eyes wasn't one of anger but of sympathy. "My mother must have suffered as well . . ." She looked away from him, across the room at the drawn curtains shutting out the street.

"Shall we sit down?" He asked this as if he'd just noticed they were standing. "Would you like a drink? I should have asked earlier. How rude of me."

"No, thank you. To both."

"Anna . . ." He sounded as if he hoped she might answer some question too complicated for him to put into words. "You're not ordinary. You're very fine."

She took a step and found herself next to him. She put her arms around him and hid her face in his neck. His arms tightened around her. She lifted her head and kissed his cheek, then his mouth, and hid her face again. But his thumb found her chin and raised it so that she had to look at him. He was smiling. She kissed his mouth a second time then rested her head on his shoulder. He held her with determination. She had arrived where she belonged.

"Anna," he said, without loosening his hold. "I'm afraid I must go." Then he released her. "I must meet with my sister, at her place. It's important I arrive on time. She's rather difficult, as you must know."

"Will you call me?"

"Of course."

Fifty-One

Nicholas startled Barbara by arriving on time. She thrust the last drawings into her portfolio, slid it under her bed, and answered the door.

"You're on time."

"Yes."

"Usually you're held up by something important," she said, a smile hovering at one corner of her mouth.

"Shall I go away and come back?"

"No, you might as well come in."

"As you like."

She poured the coffee with her left hand and passed him his cup.

"When do they take off the cast?" he asked.

"In another two weeks."

"The white makes this room seem larger. I like it."

"Thank you."

The coffee was too hot to drink. With the tip of his spoon, he pushed the granules of sugar across the bottom of the cup. There was no table beside his chair, so he set the cup on the floor.

He imagined the look of cutting disapproval Barbara would offer him if she knew he'd kissed Anna. Next, Liuba's intriguing eyes and expressive mouth formed themselves in his mind. He'd hoped to invite Liuba to the theatre for next Friday, but he hadn't called her yet. "Anna," he said to himself and he felt her hair fall against his cheek, as it had when she kissed him. A trembling delight filled him, too delicate to trust. He picked up his coffee and blew on it. There remained nothing to do but to say what he'd come to say.

"When I was eleven years old," he said, "I fell in love with Mary Bertram."

"Yes, I know."

"May I smoke?"

"I'd rather you didn't. But if you want to, go ahead."

He slipped the pack of cigarettes back into his pocket. He was in no mood to go over it all again, the bridge, the hat.

"I won't stay and trouble you for long," Nicholas said. He reached in his pocket, then held out his hand. "Here. This is for you." On his palm sat a round black box. Across the lacquered lid rode a man and a woman in a sled pulled by a single horse.

Barbara lifted the box from his hand.

"For me? Thank you. Did Liuba send you?" she asked.

"Don't do that."

"Are you lovers?"

"That's not any of your business. Ask Liuba and see what she tells you." He took out a cigarette and lighted it. "Why are you so jealous of me? What is there to be jealous of?"

"You escaped."

"Did I?"

"You've always taken what you wanted." She looked down at the box in her hand. The man and woman were wrapped in warm furs; the runners of the sled cut the hard snow; the horse galloped. "This used to be on Maman's dresser."

"Yes. And I took it."

Barbara twisted off the lid. The box was empty. Why is he

giving it to me? What will he want in exchange? She screwed the lid back on.

"When we were little, Maman used to tell us stories about them."

"The two in the sled?" asked Nicholas.

"Yes. Do you remember?"

"Of course. Who gave it to her?"

"Aunt Sonya." Barbara set the box down on her table, then picked it up again. She wanted to keep it in her palm, round and familiar. "Thank you, Nicholas," she said.

Then she turned around and saw his tears. For years, she'd wanted to make him cry. Now she felt ashamed, as though she were the cause of his pain. She started to look for a box of tissues. By the time she found one, Nicholas had taken a handkerchief from his pocket and was drying his eyes and cheeks. The look of having arrived at the end, the vulnerable exhaustion, he couldn't wipe away.

"Thank you," she said.

Nicholas returned his handkerchief to the darkness of his pocket. "You're going to send out your work, your portfolio," he said. "Mémère told me. That's splendid."

"Thank you." She looked down at the polished, round box in the palm of her hand.

Fifty-Two

THE PARIS RAIN FELL, COLD AND MERCILESS. By noon, a wind was hurling water at Mary's windows. The early summer heat of the previous days had been pounded down into the earth, deep beneath the reach of the rain.

She dialed Ivan's telephone number but there was no answer. She grabbed her umbrella and went to the zoo.

He was waiting for her at the entrance, as arranged.

"There's no point staying, is there? Not in this weather," said Mary.

"None," Ivan agreed. "May I take you somewhere, for lunch?"

She knew he had no money. "I could make you something. It wouldn't be much. But we'd be dry," she suggested.

"And you'll show me your new work?"

"If you like." He didn't ask if she'd done any new work. For him it was a given; he assumed she had. She was an artist and that was that. At such moments she felt like kissing him, out of gratitude. But he was a man and Rose's lover and so she didn't touch him but smiled her appreciation. The rain beat down on her umbrella. His shoes were wet, she noticed, the leather darkening like the day.

Mary lit both the kerosene heaters. Ivan pulled off his sodden socks and thrust his feet into the heat. It was a violent heat within a small radius, yet weak enough that it would take hours to spread through the room.

It wasn't the first time he'd come to her studio and looked at her work. But never in such weather. They'd had remarkable luck on their sketching expeditions to the zoo. The menace of rain, a few drops, but never this.

"I can't stand this weather," said Ivan. "Paris is detestable when it rains." He walked over, in his bare feet, and scrutinized her most recent painting—two faceless women, playing chess.

Mary gathered together a makeshift lunch and set it on the table. "It's not much," she told him.

"Not much?" He stepped from behind her painting, frowning. He loathed false modesty and lack of faith.

"I don't mean the painting. What I've found for our lunch isn't much," she explained.

He walked over to her. A giraffe. He moves like a giraffe, she thought.

"You'll be leaving Paris soon. When you're back in Canada, you must not stop painting." He stood close to her, perhaps because the room was cold, perhaps to give his words urgency. He smelled sour and sweet, both at once.

"How did you know I was leaving?" she asked.

"Rose told me."

"I'm running out of money," she explained. "I haven't your courage. I can't stay here forever. Besides, I'm not French."

"Neither am I," he said, then walked back to her painting and stared at it. "I won't stay either. They don't want what I'm doing."

It was always her work that claimed his attention when he came over. There weren't many men she felt like touching. Most of them bored her. She kept her thoughts to herself and smiled at them. Her beauty had come the year she turned twenty. Before that, she'd lived a plain and plump existence. She still distrusted the attention her beauty brought her.

"You're not going to marry and have children, once you're in Canada, I hope." Again he came and stood close to her. He ran his finger along her cheek and grinned. "I forbid you to let your talents go to waste."

"I'll do as I please. I'm not a child. I'm a year older than you."

"Mary."

She kissed him. Her mouth explored his; he became the sea entering every crevice of her.

The cold rain streamed down the immense windows.

Fifty-Three

It was a Sunday afternoon, and they'd been to the movies. Rose was in the kitchen, speaking with her mother, who insisted on brewing coffee for Mary and Ivan.

"*Barbara et Nicholas, ils étaient sages?*"

"They were so quiet, I did not know they were here, *ma chérie.*"

"*C'est bien.* And where are they?"

"Nicholas is in his bedroom doing his homework, and Barbara is on the balcony, I believe."

The kettle announced its readiness with a piercing whistle.

Mary's shoe had started rubbing her ankle as she left the cinema. Perched on the edge of the velvet settee, Mary slipped it off. It would be a few moments before Eugénie and Rose brought in the coffee. She bent her head and examined her ankle.

Seated beside Mary, Ivan studied the provocative purity of her white hair. Its colour demanded to be disturbed. He reached over and parted the hairs concealing the nape of her neck. He touched the tip of his finger to the uppermost tip of her spine.

Mary kept her head lowered, her fingers pressing the raw skin at the back of her ankle.

Ivan had promised himself he wouldn't touch her, certainly not in this apartment. But the memory of holding her insisted, demanded repetition. His fingers counted the knobs of bone leading down from the vulnerable base of her skull to the back of her dress.

The noise came first from the handle, then from the hinges as the balcony door opened.

Mary's head shot up, Ivan's hand fell away, Barbara stepped into the room in front of them. She stared at them, uncomprehending. Then recognition made her eyes harden.

Mary listened to the retreating pounding of Barbara's feet, the slamming of her bedroom door. Rose's footsteps emerged from the kitchen.

Mary stood up. The trembling grew inside her, spreading. I will have to tell Rose, she thought. I won't be able to pretend it never happened, to spare both of us. As if that were ever possible. I'll have to explain.

Fifty-Four

On Sunday morning, Claire came early and took Eugénie away for the day. Anna stood in the round dining room. The loose, sunlit morning flowed around her. She wanted to enjoy its aimless loveliness but she couldn't. Will Nicholas phone this morning? she wondered. Yesterday, did I horrify him when I kissed him? She picked up Eugénie's watering can and watered the plants on the mantelpiece.

She'd forced herself to make plans for the afternoon. She'd arranged to meet a girl from her Balzac course and go for a walk in the Bois de Boulogne. Later they might see a film.

The dining room was Anna's favourite room. Its roundness promised that nothing need ever come to an end. The family's napkin rings lay piled on top of each other in a shallow basket. I must memorize every detail, thought Anna. Soon I'll be going back to Canada. How did Mom feel the day she left?

But in a round room it was impossible to think about endings.

In the hallway, a key moved in the heavy lock. Anna turned.

"*Bonjour*," said Nicholas, stepping into the doorway of the dining room. "Did I startle you? I'm so sorry."

"If you're looking for Mémère, she's not here. She's gone to Claire's for the day."

"I didn't expect her to be here." Nicholas kissed Anna on either cheek. "I came to drop off my laundry, and I hoped I might find you here."

Anna saw, in the hallway behind him, a bulging white cotton bag deposited on a chair.

"It's kind of Mémère to do your laundry."

"Yes. It's kind of her. She doesn't do everything, mostly my sheets. She insists I bring those, as she has a special ironing machine. I expect she's shown it to you? She's very proud of it."

"Yes. She gave me a demonstration."

Nicholas laughed. "I meant to call you last night, but I wasn't able to."

"It's not important."

"On the contrary, it's very important. Do you have a moment? Shall we sit down and talk?"

"Yes. If you like."

He stepped aside so that she could pass in front of him into the living room. She chose the settee and Nicholas settled into an armchair facing her. He doesn't want to touch me, she thought.

"And so, how are you?" he asked.

"I'm fine, thank you, and yourself?"

This absurd formality felt to Anna like a straitjacket. But she couldn't think how to escape it.

"I'm very well." Nicholas smiled at her, amused by her irritation, and by his own need to keep her at a distance. He was accustomed to futility, to finding the humour in it. Beneath his amusement pulsated a tangle of contradictory emotions.

"It's not possible, Anna."

He got up and walked over to his grandmother's desk and picked up her glass egg. Its weight was satisfying in his hand but offered no solution. He put it down again.

"What's not possible?" she asked, tired of waiting for his next words.

"The two of us." He wanted to study her face, but Anna looked away.

She would not cry or shout at him. Not at any cost. She saw the surface of the piano, the light dancing off it.

"Will you play something for me?"

"I haven't practised in weeks. Are you sure you want me to?"

"Yes."

He selected some sheets of music from on top of the piano and sat down.

It was horrible listening to him play. The music made her want to cry. She perched on the settee, alert, waiting for him to be done.

"*Voilà*," he said at last, turning to look at her.

"Thank you."

"I shouldn't keep you any longer. You must have work to do, or other plans?"

"I'm free until this afternoon. I've finished all my papers but one."

"Bravo. So you are hard-working?"

"Not really." As he was standing, she got up also. "And you? Mémère says you've written a book but can't find a publisher?"

"Ah. That has changed." This he said with unequivocal pleasure. "Two days ago, it was accepted. The letter arrived Friday. You mustn't tell Mémère. I'll try to call her this evening or tomorrow. She'd be hurt if she knew I'd told you first. Mémère can be a bit jealous."

"I won't say a thing. Congratulations."

"*Merci. Bon.* I must be on my way."

They stood facing each other. Bright sunlight tumbled on to the jungle of plants and books, ignited the rich colours of the carpet.

"Of course, you have work to do," said Anna, with a small note of sarcasm she hadn't intended.

"I'm glad you were here," said Nicholas. "And I am especially happy you came to see the portrait."

She felt his eyes admiring her features. We're like two chess pieces, she told herself, stuck on an abandoned board.

When he'd gone, she stood in the centre of the living room, beside his piano. From the marble mantelpiece, the sober, determined boy with the short hair observed her.

Fifty-Five

Eugénie washed Nicholas's sheets. Next she ironed them in the spare room on her special machine that sat on the desk in front of the windows. All she had to do was lift the handle up and down, and adjust the position of the sheet. When they were creaseless, she removed and folded them.

Her task done, Eugénie sat on the spare bed. Opposite the bed stood the fireplace. Not since the last war had anything burned in it. Where did the story of that war begin? To whom was she to tell it? To God? He already knew the whole tale. Why speak of it at all?

We installed a small stove in the front hall, recalled Eugénie. Each day we counted out the pieces of coal. A pot of water crowned the stove at all hours. The warm water from this pot we used for washing. In the evenings, while the rest of us gathered in the meagre warmth of the ill-fed stove, Claire and Rose studied in their bedroom, wrapped in blankets and comforters, their white breath drifting above the furniture. It was difficult for them to turn the pages without letting a blanket slip. Their fingers grew numb.

Every morning, my daughters left for the university. I waited for them to return. People were herded at random, from the sidewalk into the police vans. Interrogations followed. A winnowing of the human harvest. The Germans were on every corner, posting lists of names. The names of French citizens, shot for insurrection. Esther Wiseman, who worked in the translations office, was the first of the Jews I knew to be deported, sent to a death camp.

I boiled rutabaga and listened to all that was absent from the room but present in my head, and to the steady ticking of the clock. I waited for my daughters, for the click of their key in the lock. Every day, Rose and Claire came home. Once they brought dates. They prepared an entire meal of dates and that evening I didn't scrub any rutabagas.

For me, the war had come unexpectedly. Many anticipated its outbreak, but I did not. I had refused to examine the patterns. I was by nature a dreamer. I waited for the war to end. For a time I cried at night; then I stopped crying. I made the beds and lined up for food. I listened for Rose and Claire's key in the door. We had food, of a sort. Many did not. We were alive. Hundreds and thousands were being murdered.

EUGÉNIE YAWNED. She lay down beside the freshly washed and ironed sheets. The relief of sleep lifted her out of the room. Behind, on the bed, her sore legs waited for her to return.

Fifty-Six

June 1st, 1980

Dear Mom,

I have an idea. Will you come to Paris? In a few days I'll have done my last paper. Mémère would love to see you, and there's so much I want to talk to you about.

I have a rather grave confession to make. Just before I came here, I stole an old address book of yours. I found it in among some old postcards and catalogues of art exhibits in the cupboard facing the record-player. It's small and has a red cover. On a back page, it says, "It was the fault of the rain." There's also a tiny pencil sketch of a llama's head. I think I've figured out what it refers to. I didn't have the right to take it, but if you can forgive me, possibly you'll tell me if what I have guessed is true?

I hope you'll come to Paris. Please write soon.

Love,
Anna.

Fifty-Seven

Eugénie Balashovskaya tried to pull on her stockings. Her foot was attached, as usual, to her ankle. But when she reached down, someone invisible and cruel drove a hot nail into her shoulder. She straightened up. There was her foot, just where it belonged. She folded her stockings and returned them to their place in the drawer. She would have to do without.

As she walked down the long, narrow hall, something cool and fine caressed her naked thighs. It was the silk lining of her skirt, the silk slipping across her skin. Yes, that was it. How lovely.

Fifty-Eight

IT WAS EARLY JUNE, A HUMID THURSDAY AFTERNOON, and in the stuffy back room of the Patisserie Viennoise sat only two people.

"So, you're leaving," said Barbara.

"Yes. In three months." Liuba tore the end off the slender paper tube and the sugar poured into her hot chocolate.

"It's all ending differently than I'd expected," said Barbara.

"What's ending? Not our friendship?" said Liuba.

"No. Not that. I hope," said Barbara, smiling.

"Decidedly not that," agreed Liuba.

"What's ending? I am free of the Samaritaine," Barbara explained. "And soon Anna will be gone, back to Canada. And you are leaving." Barbara twisted a strand of hair around her finger. "I thought you were going to fall in love with him."

"With Nicholas? No."

"Are you sure?"

"Perhaps I did, for twenty-four hours. Have you heard anything about your portfolio?"

"Not yet. The Theatre du Soleil is looking at it. But they warned me they don't have any openings."

The knocking of thick china, the steamy hiss of the coffee

machine, and the clatter of spoons from the kitchen quieted the beating of Barbara's heart. The calm of custard walls. One day, thought Barbara, I could meet Nicholas here. If he'd make the time. If he wanted to.

"Still, they're looking at your work. That's a lot," said Liuba.

"Yes. And in three months you'll be gone, and I'll miss you."

"Will you come to visit?"

"Perhaps. I'd like to. How is your mother?"

"For the moment, well. I didn't think she'd agree to go with me. When she said yes, I sat there staring at her."

"She may continue to surprise you. Mémère, on the other hand, is not moving anywhere. She stubbed her big toe on her right foot, and it isn't healing. We shouldn't be surprised but we're shocked—my aunt and I. Like fools, we expect her to continue forever."

"Has her doctor prescribed anything?"

"Yes, but she won't take it. She says that her thinking is responsible, and that the other culprit is the unyielding leg of the dining room chair. I've argued with her. I wish she would take her medicine. I don't care if she has to go against her crazy beliefs. I just want her toe to heal."

"Will you introduce me to her? I've heard so much about her."

"Of course. I promise. Before you leave. Imagine, California! A land of freedom and pleasure. I hope your mother won't miss her comforting grey weather? Do they have miserable weather in San Francisco?"

"I expect so. But there's the ocean and it is dramatic, the way the city holds on to the hillside. And the members of the department, those that I've met, didn't strike me as impossible to work with and I'll have more money and greater freedom in my research."

"You are moving to the United States of America. You will have a right to happiness!"

"*Eh oui!* . . . Are you working on any new costumes?"

"Yes. For Anouilh's *Antigone*."

Liuba consulted her watch. Barbara admired the fragile bones of her wrist, then lifted her gaze to Liuba's heedless, too-wide mouth, the black layers of brightness in her eyes.

"I should be going," said Liuba. "Can I offer you a ride?"

"I've got my car," said Barbara.

"I'm sorry about Nicholas," said Liuba. She cocked her ear but heard no beating wings in anyone's chest.

"Don't be," said Barbara. "Nothing happened. And even if it had...."

"No. Something did happen," said Liuba.

"What?"

"I don't know. But something has happened, don't you think?"

"Yes. Something has happened."

"For better or for worse?" asked Liuba.

"We'll find out. Listen:"

> Valkyries are flying, the violins sing,
> The bulky opera's finale nears;
> Flunkies burdened with heavy furs,
> Await their masters on marble stairs.

"Excellent. You've learned it."

"The start. The first few lines."

"That's wonderful, you'll have to stop me from forgetting mine. I hope you'll write? And before I leave, you are going to introduce me to your grandmother."

"I promise."

Fifty-Nine

There they go, thought Eugénie. Goldfish, gliding through the murk of my father's pond. Look. Do you see the sun on their scales?

Eugénie opened her eyes and lifted her heavy head. She saw a woman seated across the table from her, her grey hair chopped short as a boy's.

"Claire, how long have I been sleeping?"

"Not long, Maman. Not more than ten minutes."

"Are you leaving now?"

"No. Not yet. Léon will pick me up at three-thirty."

"Good. Then I will see him, also."

How lovely her eyes are, thought Eugénie. They are gathering everything in the room for her mind to arrange. I have a splendid daughter. I used to have two daughters. She closed her eyes and tried arranging the goldfish in rows, but they slipped between the weeds. Shall I follow them? The water looks refreshing. But it is muddy. I mustn't get my shoes dirty. She looked down. There was a streak of dirt on her stocking and the toes of her shoes were caked with muck. I must clean it off, she thought, before my nanny sees. The goldfish are like flames, fallen into the pond. Isn't the sun dazzling today?

EUGÉNIE OPENED HER EYES. Claire was peeling an orange. The peel fell in a curl onto Claire's plate. Someone was playing a cello. Volodya, no doubt. The notes climbed up and down the backs of the chairs. Eugénie saw them straddling the bars. Could Claire see them? How vigorous Volodya's playing was today.

"Claire, you are not leaving yet?"

"Not yet. Shall I pour you some more coffee?"

"Yes, please. And a piece of chocolate. I feel like eating a morsel of chocolate, today. There is a bar in the kitchen, *ma chérie*, in the cupboard facing the back door. Would you mind bringing it? I keep it for Nicholas. Do you think he'll mind if a mouse has been at it?"

"He may buy you a cat."

Eugénie's laugh rumbled the length of the mantelpiece and vanished beneath the leaves of the wandering jew.

Claire went to fetch Nicholas's chocolate bar.

NOW WHITE CLOUDS floated in the pond, and the goldfish swam through them. Why, the fish are gliding through the branches of the trees, thought Eugénie. Look, look! Claire, do come and see! Hurry—soon it will be over. There is a breeze swaying the branches and the goldfish are darting in between. How brilliant the sun is today!

Have I fallen into the pond? I'm swallowing water. Why is it so hard to breathe? Look, the sun is setting fire to the fish. Do come quickly, Claire. I must get some air. Claire, you must see, you must, the sun has set fire to the fish.

ALL THIS TRAVELLING back and forth to Maman's, thought Claire, returning with the bar of chocolate. And her toe isn't healing. I should probably be coming every day instead of every other day. She set Nicholas's chocolate on the table. Eugénie was sleeping, her chin resting on her chest. In the stillness of the room, Claire sat down at her place.

The part in Maman's hair isn't straight, she thought, studying her mother's tilted head. She got up and chose a pear from the cheerful Moroccan bowl on the sideboard. The deep, old drawer squealed as she pulled it open to take out a fruit knife, but the noise didn't wake her mother. The knife was small. She looked at the pretty handle, made of mother-of-pearl. There's so much I don't pay attention to. Maman would tell me my thinking is wrong. She cut her yellow pear in half. Then she looked across the dining room table and understood that her mother was dead.

The room felt still, despite the noises of the street. Somewhere the cars continued. A shovel scraped across gravel, far away. It all continued, far away.

You died alone, while I was in the kitchen getting a chocolate bar, thought Claire. And this thought stood out, purposeless as the furniture in the room. What use are chairs with no one to sit in them? she wondered. Yet the chairs looked beautiful in the sunlight. She realized she hadn't really looked at the chairs in years. You died by yourself, in the sunlight; while I was in the kitchen getting a chocolate bar.

How do I know she's dead? Claire came around the table and lifted her mother's wrist. Yes. There was no mistake, no reason to hope. Where have you gone? Don't leave, she felt like screaming. Don't go. Not yet. We didn't say goodbye. Please, tell me where you are! But Eugénie did not open her large, blue eyes and say, "Here I am. Don't be frightened, *ma chérie*. I am here. I will always be here." Instead, Claire listened to the knocking of her own heart, the obscene, joyous, hungry flowing of blood inside herself.

She walked into the living room and picked up the glass egg that held down the papers on her mother's desk. She carried the egg with her, from plant to bookshelf to piano. I should speak to someone, she thought. At last, Maman is resting. She didn't want to live much longer. Claire tasted salt and realized that tears were running down her cheeks. I must telephone Léon.

She arrived at the telephone and sat down, Eugénie's glass egg in her lap. She dialed, then looked through the doors into the round dining room. There slumped her mother as if dozing, as if digesting her meal.

Sixty

At five o'clock, when Anna slipped her key into the lock and opened the door, she was greeted by Léon. "Anna, may I speak with you in your room?"

"Of course." Mémère is dead; Mémère has died. How do I know? wondered Anna.

The certainty of Eugénie's death made everything stop, in the hallway and inside herself. Nothing preceding this moment of certainty, and nothing yet to come, mattered.

Anna glanced in the direction of the sitting room. She saw Claire's back and, half-hidden, Eugénie's legs as she lay on her blue Mitterrand. If Mémère were ill, she would not be on the couch but in an ambulance.

Anna walked with Léon down the long corridor to her room, and she opened her door.

"Sit down, *ma chère* Anna."

Anna did as she was told.

"Mémère has died?" she asked.

"Yes. She is dead. Her life ended this afternoon in the most peaceful way possible. She had eaten lunch with Claire. When Claire returned from the kitchen, her mother was in her chair at the table, just as before, but her heart had stopped."

"She must have been very tired."

"She lived a long life. There were few pleasures left for her."

"Do Nicholas and Barbara know?"

"I called them both but couldn't reach either of them. I will try again later."

"And how is Claire?"

"She knew it must happen. But she didn't expect it."

"Poor Claire."

"Yes."

"Will they come and take Mémère away?"

"Her doctor should arrive any minute. He will certify her death—the obvious, but it must be done. Next they will come from the funeral home. I must leave you. I want to be there when the doctor arrives."

"Of course. Thank you, Léon."

He took Anna in his arms and held her. The strength of his arms surprised her. Then he hurried down the corridor.

ANNA SAT ON HER BED, staring at the faded blue silk that covered the walls of her room. A sudden excitement ran through her. Everything is over, she thought. At last, something new can begin. Something clean and truly novel. But she looked out the window, and there was the thick, grey wall of the balcony, a sparrow hopping along it. She was not going to soar into a world that was clean and new. Rather, she was standing on the lip of a dark pit.

Is there nothing left of you, Mémère? But whom was she asking? Herself. And she did not know the answer. I'll never hear your laugh again, thought Anna. It's unfair. It's unbearable. Whose room is this now? Whom does my room belong to?

She wanted to telephone her mother. It would not yet be noon in Toronto. She imagined Nicholas, sobbing, covering his face with his hands, and felt ashamed because she also imagined putting her arms around him and comforting him. She got up and opened the door onto her thin strip of balcony. The sparrow flew away.

LATER LÉON KNOCKED on her door to say he was heating some soup. She went in and ate with them. Mémère's body was gone. She'd wanted to come out earlier, but she hadn't dared.

Shortly after ten, Léon knocked on her door again. He said he and Claire were leaving and would she like to spend the night at their house? But Anna didn't want to leave. She didn't think Claire wanted to leave either, but that Léon had decided what was best. But that's none of my business, she thought.

When they'd left, Anna closed the apartment door and walked to her room. Directly across the narrow corridor stood the door to Eugénie's bedroom, closed. She opened it and flicked on the light. The small white sink shone and the dark bulk of the wardrobe filled the other corner. The bed looked small, its brown cover old and dull. I shouldn't be violating Mémère's privacy, staring at her bed. Anna flicked off the light and closed the door.

The narrow corridor opened into the expansive hall. She crossed the Persian carpets. In the living room, she passed the tangle of plants and books that threatened to topple the round table. She passed Nicholas's piano, then Eugénie's desk. The glass egg was gone.

Anna opened the door onto the balcony and stepped out. On the far side of the river, the Eiffel Tower was dressed up for the night in its orange light.

After the funeral, thought Anna, Mom will come, or possibly in time for it. Then she and I will leave Paris for the countryside. We'll walk along some wooded lane together, or beside the ocean, and get to know each other. Mom loves the ocean. Anna wiped her eyes on the back of her hand. She hadn't expected to be crying, not so soon again.

The cars were crossing the bridge, their headlights

unblinking. The summer air brushed her cheek, and far below, it slipped between the leaves of the trees along the river.

Anna imagined Nicholas was standing beside her. He offered her his handkerchief. He asked her not to leave Paris, to stay with him forever. Haven't I learned a thing? Anna asked herself. She went indoors, shutting the balcony doors behind her.